Rafe Was U...
Trying To S...

wanting something from
playing the game, he prided himself on being one
of the best, making certain first that everyone knew
the rules.

Molly probably didn't even know there *were* rules.

She smiled at him. When she forgot herself long
enough, she was surprisingly attractive. Friendly,
warm, engaging…pretty.

Pretty? Hell, she looked beautiful!

But what was *he* going to do about it?

Dear Reader,

Welcome to the world of Silhouette Desire, where you can indulge yourself every month with romances that can only be described as passionate, powerful and provocative!

Fabulous BJ James brings you June's MAN OF THE MONTH with *A Lady for Lincoln Cade*. In promising to take care of an ex-flame—and the widow of his estranged friend— Lincoln Cade discovers she has a child. Bestselling author Leanne Banks offers another title in her MILLION DOLLAR MEN miniseries with *The Millionaire's Secret Wish*. When a former childhood sweetheart gets amnesia, a wealthy executive sees his chance to woo her back.

Desire is thrilled to present another exciting miniseries about the scandalous Fortune family with FORTUNES OF TEXAS: THE LOST HEIRS. Anne Marie Winston launches the series with *A Most Desirable M.D.*, in which a doctor and nurse share a night of passion that leads to marriage! Dixie Browning offers a compelling story about a sophisticated businessman who falls in love with a plain, plump woman while stranded on a small island in *More to Love*. Cathleen Galitz's *Wyoming Cinderella* features a young woman whose life is transformed when she becomes nanny to the children of her brooding, rich neighbor. And Kathie DeNosky offers her hero a surprise when he discovers a one-night stand leads to pregnancy and true love in *His Baby Surprise*.

Indulge yourself with all six Desire titles—and see details inside about our exciting new contest, "Silhouette Makes You a Star."

Enjoy!

Joan Marlow Golan

Joan Marlow Golan
Senior Editor, Silhouette Desire

Please address questions and book requests to:
Silhouette Reader Service
U.S.: 3010 Walden Ave., P.O. Box 1325, Buffalo, NY 14269
Canadian: P.O. Box 609, Fort Erie, Ont. L2A 5X3

More to Love
DIXIE BROWNING

Published by Silhouette Books
America's Publisher of Contemporary Romance

To all of us "generous" women

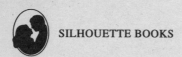

SILHOUETTE BOOKS

ISBN 0-373-76372-7

MORE TO LOVE

Visit Silhouette at www.eHarlequin.com

Printed in U.S.A.

DIXIE BROWNING

has been writing for Silhouette since 1980 and recently celebrated the publication of her sixty-fifth book, *Texas Millionaire*. She has also written a number of historical romances with her sister under the name Bronwyn Williams. An award-winning painter and writer, Browning lives on the Outer Banks of North Carolina. You can write to her at P.O. Box 1389, Buxton, NC 27920.

One

To think she had actually considered slipping peacefully into a midlife crisis, never mind that according to one article she had read there was no such thing. She'd had all the classic symptoms. Worry about her looks, about broken relationships and career disappointments, about the waning importance to her family.

Besides, the alternative seemed so selfish. Wanting something for herself.

But a midlife crisis? At the age of thirty-six? Hardly. And Annamarie was still depending on her, which was the reason she was here. As for her new career, it looked promising, once the electricians and painters and plasterers got finished so that everyone could move in again. Being head housekeeper in an assisted-living home might not be the most glamorous career in the world, but then, Molly was nothing if not a realist. And she was finally doing something about her looks. As for the other symptom—the relationship thing—her one shot at happy-ever-after had given her a genuine distaste for fairy tales.

Only four days ago Molly had caught her first glimpse of the ocean. She had seen a sand dune that was almost as big as one of her own West Virginia mountains. She had collected a bushel of tourist brochures on her way down the Outer Banks, telling herself she would read every one and see everything that looked halfway interesting.

And it all did. The miracle was that for once in her life she had time on her hands. The only thing she had to do was feed and water a couple of birds and clean their cages, and look after one elderly cat.

The ferry ride from Hatteras to Ocracoke had been just the beginning. There was an observation deck, but as it had taken her about twenty minutes of the allotted forty to work up enough nerve to step out of her car, she had never made it up the narrow ladder. Instead she'd grabbed hold of the metal railing and waited to see if she was going to be sick. It had taken a few more minutes to get used to the gentle rolling motion of the deck, but there was so much to take in that she'd soon forgotten all about her queasiness. Flocks of seagulls following the ferry swooped down to catch scraps of bread tossed by three pretty girls standing at the chain across the stern. They passed another ferry headed in the opposite direction, and people waved. Feeling bold and adventurous, Molly released her grip on the railing and waved back.

It had to be fate, she remembered thinking at the time. First, the lightning strike that had caused Holly Hills Home where she worked to be shut down for repairs. Next, the fact that Stu and Annamarie had rented a cottage on Ocracoke Island and then decided to take a week off for a side trip and needed someone to look after Pete, Repete and Shag. Molly couldn't remember the last time she had taken a real vacation. She hadn't even had to think twice when Annamarie called to ask if there was any possible way she could come down and take care of the critters for just a few days. It was only a five-hour drive, one way. Ferry included.

Molly had gone right out and splurged on three new outfits suitable for a beach vacation in late April. If she could have found a T-shirt that said Live For The Moment, or Go With The Flow, she would probably have bought it, never mind that she was built more for tents and tunics than T-shirts.

She remembered singing "Don't Worry, Be Happy" under her breath as she'd stood there on the ferry watching the water of Hatteras Inlet flow past. Where better than an island to adopt that attitude?

The teenage girls had giggled and postured. They were a bit underdressed for the weather, which was still cool. But then, if she'd had their figures she might have done some showing off, too. The ferry had been loaded with fishermen, some of them young and attractive. A few were asleep in their vehicles, a few more were outside comparing fishing gear. Most were watching the girls, except for one who was— mercy, he looked like a young Sly Stallone!—watching her!

Watching *her?*

Pretending she hadn't noticed, Molly concentrated on a big black bird sitting on a post out in the water, his wings spread as if he were about to take off.

"Cormorant," said the Stallone look-alike, edging closer along the railing. "Drying his wings." Up close, he was only a few inches taller than Molly's modest five foot two, and already he was showing signs of a beer belly, but he had a nice smile.

She glanced up at the cloudless sky, then back at Sleepy Eyes. "How did they get wet?"

"Diving for dinner."

She remembered trying to look as if she knew precisely what he meant, but as the whole experience had been so new, she probably hadn't been too convincing.

"First time down here?" he asked.

"Actually, it is."

"Me, I come every year, spring and fall. Me and my buddies enter tournaments all up and down the coast. The weather can turn on you real quick this time of year, though. You shoulda waited a few weeks."

"Fishing tournaments?"

He pointed to the small pennant flying from the antenna of his dark green pickup truck. "O.I.F.T. That's Ocracoke International or Invitational, anyway you want to call it." He went on to describe several such tournaments and his prowess at each while Molly soaked up the novelty of sunshine and seagulls, a moving deck underfoot and the full attention, for the moment at least, of a handsome young man. Could someone have waved a magic wand, turning plain, plump Molly Dewhurst into someone her own mirror wouldn't recognize? Had the lumbering old ferryboat been a pumpkin in a previous incarnation?

"Cut bait's what you want. Some like bloodworms, but me, I like salt mullet best."

All right, so his charm was a little on the rustic side. No one had ever accused her of being a snob.

Reaching into the back of his truck, he took a can of beer from the cooler, offered it to Molly, and when she refused, popped the top and drained half the contents in one thirsty gulp.

Molly fingered a strand of blowing hair away from her eyes. Sunglasses. She should have thought to get herself a pair. Big ones. Then she could ogle all she wanted to without getting caught at it. She'd invested in a new lipstick, a new hairstyle and the new outfits, but spending money on herself took practice. She hadn't quite got the knack of it yet.

"Where you staying?" he drawled. He had one of those raspy voices that went with his sleepy eyes.

Molly swallowed hard and tried to sound terribly blasé. "It's a cottage. My sister's. Actually it's not hers. She's only renting it."

"So maybe I'll see you around?" Was that an opening or a dismissal?

She took several mental steps back. She didn't do casual flirtations. The old Molly had never had a chance to learn, and the new Molly needed to work on self-confidence first. "Maybe so," she said airily. "If I don't see you again, good luck in the tournament."

"When it comes to fishing, I make my own luck." He flashed her a lazy grin. "There's sixty teams in this one, with a mile-long waiting list. If you're a betting woman, put your money on ol' Jeffy Smith."

"Thank you. I'll, uh—do that." Molly remembered thinking at the time that men based their ego on the strangest things. Her ex-husband, for instance, made certain everyone knew he'd gone to Yale, never mind that he'd lasted only a single semester. Jeffy Smith evidently took pride in his prowess as a fisherman—or maybe in being a member of an exclusive group. But he'd been friendly. He'd seemed nice. He was attractive in a rough sort of way. And as she had recently cast off her old persona, determined to take a cue from a recruiting slogan and become all she could become, she'd responded with a smile.

And then Jeffy had tossed his beer can over the side, patted his belly and belched. So much for her ferryboat Prince Charming. He was obviously a man's man. But then, she'd reminded herself, her ex-husband had been a ladies' man. Of the two, she preferred the slob.

Correction. Of the two, she preferred neither. Still, it was a shame. Her very first shipboard romance, and it had ended before it even began.

"We'll be landing in a couple of minutes. Now, remember, if you need any help learning how to hold a rod, you just call on ol' Jeffy." His eyes had twinkled. He had black eyes, black hair and a three-days' growth of beard. Molly hadn't known if it was a fashion statement or one of those things men did when they were off the reservation. With Kenny, it had been just the opposite. When he was home, he never bothered to shave or even comb his hair, but if he'd been going out anywhere at all, it was full-dress parade, from the fancy designer shoes he had charged to her account to the expensive cologne he splashed on his throat before he buttoned his designer shirt and knotted his designer tie.

Once when he'd gone on and on about designer this and designer that, she'd asked him who designed the clothes that didn't bear a designer's label. He'd given her a blank stare and asked for fifty dollars to tide him over.

That was another thing about Kenny Dewhurst. He was totally devoid of a sense of humor. He was equally devoid of any funds except those provided by his doormat of a wife.

Ex-doormat, Molly remembered thinking. Breathing deeply of freedom, diesel fumes and salt air, she had smiled at the semi-handsome slob leaning on the railing beside her while the heavy engines throbbed beneath her feet. Here she was, under a cloudless blue sky, off on an island adventure, and before she even set foot on the island, a friendly man had struck up a conversation with her while only a few feet away three really cute girls, size zilch, were flirting with his fishing buddies.

The engines had changed pitch as the ferry swerved into a narrow channel. Her Stallone look-alike had said, "Guess I'd better load up. So…I guess I'll see you around, huh?"

"Probably. I understand it's a small island." *Nice going, Molly. Not too eager, not too cool.* She had climbed back into her car and watched through the rearview mirror as he rejoined his friends. There were some knowing grins, a few elbows to the ribs, and then they stowed their gear and climbed into their muscle trucks.

"Stowed their gear," she repeated smugly now. Pretty nautical for a woman who had never before set foot on an island. Never even set foot outside West Virginia until four months ago.

She was going to like this new Molly just fine. She had…well, maybe not style. At least not yet. But she had attitude, by heck, and that was the first step!

* * *

That had been four days ago. That very afternoon Stu and Annamarie had caught the last ferry headed north, after writing detailed instructions on how to care for the two African Gray parrots and Shag the cat. The next morning Molly had introduced herself to the next-door neighbor, Sally Ann Haskins, who told her how to find the general store, the post office, and tried to tempt her into taking a puppy off her hands.

"Mama Dog's plumb worn out. I'm going to get her fixed. She had seven this time. Last time it was eleven, poor thing. You sure you couldn't use a nice retriever pup? Your sister said she had too many animals already, but she said you might be interested."

"I'd love one, but—" Mama Dog flapped her tail lethargically, but didn't even lift her head when Molly knelt and reached for one of her squirming babies. "But the place where I live has this rule about animals."

"Reckon I could offer it as a prize in the fishing tournament? Biggest catch of the day gets a free puppy? Fishermen mostly drive pickup trucks, and every pickup has to have a dog to ride in the back. It's a state law."

So then Molly had told her all about the ferryboat encounter with a fisherman in a dogless pickup truck. "Just when I was starting to think he had real possibilities, he threw his beer can overboard."

"You know the old saying, garbage in, garbage out." Sally Ann worked for the ferry department, which Molly considered wildly exciting. "Maybe the jerk'll hook into his own beer can and wreck his gear. They say there's a big low headed up the coast. Last three years in a row, the weather's been so bad, most folks left after the first day. You don't want to try surf fishing in gale force winds—the sand'll cut the skin right off your face.''

"Mercy. Why not schedule it for when the weather's better?''

"You know anybody that can schedule the weather? They set it for when the fish are supposed to be here.'' Sally Ann finished ironing a uniform shirt, unplugged the iron and plopped it on the kitchen range to cool. "Trouble is, if the weather closes in, they wait until too late to get off the island. Once the highway's flooded, they're stuck with nothing better to do than shoot pool and tell lies about the big one that got away.''

"Still, it doesn't sound like good planning to me.''

Sally grinned. A strawberry blonde, she had a weathered face, perfect teeth and the biggest, bluest eyes Molly had ever seen. "Makes for some fun, though. Socializing's a big part of these tournaments. If the weather shuts down and they get tired of baling hay, they head for the pubs. And let me tell you, if this low hangs around too long, there'll be some hot old times down at Delroy's Pub.''

One hand on the doorknob, Molly paused. "Uh— did you say baling hay? I thought they were fishing?''

"Catching eelgrass. With the water so rough, the bottom's all tore up. Seaweed's about all they haul in.''

The next day dark clouds closed in, bringing stiff winds that tore new leaves from ancient trees and set small boats to bobbing like corks at the wharf. It was raining, but not heavily when Molly left the general store with a sack of apples and headed back to the cottage. Rain or shine, she was determined to walk each day as part of her new regime.

Diet and exercise. Ugh! Traffic had tripled since she'd arrived only a few days ago. Idly she wondered what had happened to her ferryboat acquaintance. Had he left? Was he shooting pool and swapping lies, or fishing in the rain?

The fish wouldn't know if it was raining or not…would they?

Remembering Sally Anne's warning, that he might try to score a little something on the side just to make the trip worthwhile, she had to laugh. It was flattering to think a warning would even be necessary. The new Molly must be coming along faster than she'd thought, if she had to worry about men trying to pick her up.

"Hi there, pretty lady."

Molly nearly dropped her apples as the familiar-looking dark green truck pulled up beside her. "Oh, hi. How's fishing, uh—Jeffy?"

"Tournament's over. We drew a lousy spot this year, but at least I didn't get skunked. I'm staying on a few more days, long's I come all this way—headed out now to look over conditions. With the wind like this, the beach'll get cut up some. Might be a few promising new sloughs. Wanna come along for the ride?"

A small voice in the back of her mind whispered, *"Watch it, lady, you might've shed a few pounds, but you're not ready for prime time yet."*

The old Molly was aghast to hear the new Molly say cheerfully, "Well…sure, why not?" She accepted the callused hand and hauled herself up into the high cab. So he was something of a slob. So his grammar wasn't perfect and he belched and tossed beer cans. Back in Grover's Hollow some of the nicest people she knew probably did the same thing when no one was looking. But he was friendly, and after all, she wasn't committing herself to anything more than a drive along the beach, which she certainly couldn't do in her own car.

Rarely did Rafe Webber find himself in an awkward situation, thanks to excellent instincts and an impeccable sense of timing. On the few occasions when he blundered, he usually managed to finesse his way out with the minimum amount of damage. This time things might be different. His instincts had been signaling trouble ever since Stu had called to tell him he was getting married to the most beautiful, brilliant, wonderful woman in the world. Rafe had strongly advised a cooling-off period, meaning, *wait until I have time to check things out, little buddy.* Unfortunately Stu had been too charged up to listen.

Rafe had been on his way out of the country at the time. He'd been held up a lot longer than he'd expected, missing Thanksgiving and Christmas completely. Not that he was sentimental—no way! Still, he'd always made a point of getting together for holidays, just to give the kid a sense of stability. He'd read somewhere that establishing traditions helped ground rebellious adolescents, which Stu had been when Rafe had first got him. For the past ten years, Rafe always cooked his special turkey dinner, regardless of the holiday.

So he'd missed the wedding, too. By the time he made it back to the States, the deed was done. But tomorrow was the kid's birthday, and regardless of

the bride and an inconvenient nor'easter, he wasn't
going to miss that. He'd checked the weather when
he'd filed his flight plan. Two separate low-pressure
areas were due to join forces just off the North Carolina coast, but he figured he had plenty of time to
slide on in before the weather closed in. What he
hadn't figured on was finding the whole damned island foundering under a load of surf fishermen. While
it might be good for business, it was a damned nuisance when a guy got in late, needing a decent rental
car and a room for a couple of days.

Before leaving Pelican's Cove, Florida, Rafe had
cleared his calendar for a week, even though he figured it would take only a couple of days to make
things up to the kid and find out how much trouble
he'd gotten himself in. Not to mention what it was
going to take to get him out of it. Stu's taste in
women was notorious. From the time Rafe had taken
over the care and feeding of a freckle-faced adolescent with too much money, too many hormones and
too little common sense, Stu had been a target for
every predatory female in range.

This one had waited until Rafe was headed out of
the country on a little unofficial business for the government and then reeled in her catch. Stuart Mont-
gomery Grainger III. Old family, new money. Gull-
ible Grainger, green as his daddy's billions. Rafe had
dared hope that, with a college degree and a brand-
new teaching job waiting for him, his half brother
might have matured enough to be let off the leash.
The lady had outsmarted him. She'd sprung her trap
before any of the family had had a chance to check
her out. Not that anyone besides Rafe would even
bother, unless it was Stu's father's lawyers.

Ten years ago Rafe's mother had dropped in out of the blue with a scared, resentful fifteen-year-old in tow and announced that as the two of them were half brothers, it was time they got to know one another. To say Rafe was appalled would be an understatement. The only thing that had kept him from flat-out refusing was the fact that the kid obviously felt the same way. Rafe could remember all too well how he'd felt at that age, being shunted between summer camp and boarding school so as not to cramp his mother's lifestyle.

They'd spent the next five years getting to know each other, with Rafe trying his damnedest to instill a few survival instincts in a kid who hadn't a clue.

Evidently he hadn't succeeded. Those wedding pictures that had been waiting when he'd finally made it back to the States had pretty much told the story. Gorgeous bride wearing a knock-out gown, grinning groom wearing cake on his face. The kid still looked about fifteen. You had to wonder if the bride would have been so determined to tie the knot if his name had been Joe Jones instead of S. M. Grainger III of the shipping and banking Graingers.

About all Rafe could do at this point was damage control. Fly in unannounced, apologize for missing out on all the festivities and cook Stu his favorite holiday dinner, which happened to be the only family-style dinner Rafe knew how to prepare. It would serve as a birthday treat, a reminder to Stu that he had family standing squarely behind him, and a similar warning to the bride. It would also tell him a lot about this paragon the kid had married. If she could be bought off, he'd be better off without her.

Rafe wondered how much Stu had told her about

his wildly dysfunctional family. There was the father who couldn't be bothered to keep in touch. The mother who sent extravagant birthday gifts on the wrong date. Somewhere there were some half siblings who might or might not know him personally—not to mention a big brother who had invested a lot of years into keeping him on the right track.

At the moment Rafe was more concerned with the woman. On the way north he had settled on a test he used often in business: the element of surprise. Setting things up, then observing the way people reacted to the unexpected. Having a stranger drop in out of the blue with an armload of groceries to commandeer a woman's kitchen might not be quite as effective a test as being stranded together in a leaky cabin cruiser, but it should do the trick. He could hardly come right out and ask the bride if she was more interested in the trust fund Stu stood to inherit at the age of thirty-one, or the shy, good-natured guy with a good mind, a heart of gold but damned few social skills.

While he secured the plane, taking extra precautions against the wind, Rafe ran through a few old chestnuts about brothers' keepers and no man being an island in an effort to rationalize his guilty conscience for having dropped out of sight at a time when Stu had needed him. He didn't do guilt well. When he'd found out the honeymooners would be spending a few months on one of the islands off the North Carolina coast, it had seemed like the perfect chance to mend a few fences and at the same time see how much trouble Stu was in with this bride of his and what it was going to take to sort things out. Happy marriages did not run in their family.

Unfortunately marriage did. Stella, the mother they

shared, had been married four times to date. A six-foot-tall ex-Vegas showgirl, she was still a beautiful woman at age fifty-nine-and-holding.

Rafe's father had been married three times to successively younger women, and was currently working out prenuptials with number four. Probably a high school cheerleader this time. Rafe didn't know about Stu's old man, but figured he was probably in the same league, marriagewise.

It was when Stella had been about to set out on honeymoon number three a few days before Thanksgiving that she'd turned up at the door of Rafe's condo with the kid. Once he'd gotten over the shock of finding himself unexpectedly landed with the care and feeding of a half-grown boy, Rafe had scrambled like crazy not to blow it. He'd canceled a nine-day trip to Vancouver with Linda—or maybe it had been Liz. He had taken a crash course in basic cooking and started reading every book on adolescent psychology he could lay his hands on. Over the next few years they had weathered countless minor mishaps and a few major ones. He liked the kid.

Hell, he loved the kid.

He'd done a good job of raising him, too, if he did say so himself. Stu was no athlete—they'd both reluctantly faced that fact after half a dozen or so spectacular failures. He was a fine young man, smart as a whip when it came to books. Trouble was, he was dumb as a stump where women were concerned.

That was where Rafe had always come in. Sifting the wheat from the chaff, so to speak. Unfortunately it had mostly been chaff up to now, but at least he'd managed to keep Stu out of major trouble until the call had come a couple of months ago. Rafe had been

within hours of leaving the country on another unofficial fact-finding trip. As a small-time Gulf Coast
resort developer with a modest charter boat fleet, he
had the perfect excuse to explore the coastal regions
of Central and South America. Having served a hitch
in the Coast Guard before Stu had come to live with
him, he was well aware of the fact that DEA was
undermanned, underfunded and overwhelmed.

Which was how he'd happened to miss the wedding. Thanks to a small misunderstanding with a
bunch of entrepreneurs in a little fishing village in
Central America, he'd been out of circulation for the
next several weeks, but at least he was going to make
the kid's twenty-fifth birthday.

What he hadn't figured on was the size of Ocracoke
Island in relation to the concentration of tourists.
Wall-to-wall fishermen, according to the fellow
who'd driven the rental out to the airport to meet him.
He should have made advance reservations, in case
the honeymoon cottage lacked a guest room.

The airport was little more than a paved landing
strip with a phone booth and an open pavilion, all
within a few hundred yards of the Atlantic. It was
crowded and exposed, but adequate. He'd seen a lot
worse. Knowing the weather was likely to deteriorate
before the low moved offshore again, he took his time
with the tie-downs and chocks. Hatteras Lows were
notorious, even in Florida. Once he was satisfied, he
slung his gear, which included several large grocery
sacks, into the only available rental vehicle, an SUV
with a gutted muffler and rusted-out floorboards.

He dropped the driver off at the rental place after
learning the location of Yaupon Cottage and roughly
how to find it, and toyed with the notion of checking

into a hotel first. He decided against it. The turkey needed to go into an oven, or else they'd be lucky to dine before midnight. And while that didn't bother him at all, Stu and whatsername might have other ideas.

Mission underplanned.

Traffic was bumper-to-bumper. Locating Yaupon Cottage wasn't quite as easy as it had sounded. The village was laid out as if someone had tossed handsful of confetti into the air and then built something wherever a scrap of paper landed. With the low cloud cover, there was barely enough light left to see his way up and down the narrow, winding roads with vehicles parked haphazardly on both sides.

He managed to find the place, and then had to squeeze in between a picket fence and a tan sedan. By then the rain had started coming down in solid, wind-driven sheets. Hatless, coatless, he jogged up the path to the front door and knocked. And then he pounded again and waited. There was no light on inside. It might not be wise to walk in unannounced on a honeymoon couple, but dammit, his backside was getting wet. The grocery sacks were melting. So he pounded a few more times, then tried the doorknob. Finding the door unlocked, he opened it and called, ''Hey, kids? Stu? Anybody home?''

Two

Dammit, they couldn't be too far away, or else they'd have locked the place. Pushing the door open, Rafe shoved the groceries and his battered leather bag in out of the rain. He should have called first. He should have called before he'd ever left Florida.

Too late now. After a quick look around, he set to work on the surprise birthday dinner. He preferred to think of it as that rather than as a test for the bride, but he was beginning to have a funny feeling about this whole affair. If things didn't work out, Stu was going to take it hard. From some unknown ancestor, the kid had inherited the genes for vulnerability and sensitivity. Thank God those had skipped Rafe. If there were two things he was not, it was vulnerable and sensitive.

The place was a dump. If there was a level surface anywhere, it wasn't easily discernible. It was small to the point of claustrophobic, and the two refrigerator-size birdcages in the room across the hall didn't help. Stu had mentioned that his bride had a couple of birds. Rafe had pictured budgies. Maybe canaries.

Through the open door, he eyed the two red-tailed gray parrots in the next room. Tilting their heads, they eyed him back. Feeling vaguely self-conscious, he turned his attention back to the turkey he'd bought in Tampa and allowed to thaw on the way north. He probably should've opted for something simpler, but the grand gesture had been part of the plan. Showing up with deli food and a bottle of wine wouldn't do the trick. It had been his experience that wives didn't care much for surprises, and a raw turkey definitely qualified as a surprise.

Rafe had had a wife of his own, briefly. He'd like to think Stu would have better luck, but he wouldn't bet on it. Marital bliss was not a component of their gene pool, on either the maternal or the paternal side, he reminded himself as he rummaged underneath the counter for a roasting pan. If the kid found himself married to the wrong kind of woman, who better than Rafe to lead him out of the wilderness?

Judging strictly from the wedding pictures that had been waiting in his stack of mail when he'd gotten back from his extended stay in Central America, the lady was gorgeous and at least three inches taller than her bridegroom, who'd been grinning like Howdy Doody in every single picture. Knowing Stu, Rafe figured his half brother probably hadn't bothered to draw up a prenuptial agreement.

Knowing women in general, the bride probably would have talked him out of it even if he had. His baby brother all but carried a sign that said Kick Me.

The range was an ancient model, the oven barely big enough to hold a roasting pan and the sweet potato casserole he'd planned. In the years after Stu had gone off to college, Rafe's cooking had been limited to intimate dinners for two, usually followed by breakfast. Other than that, he ate out. Domestic, he was not. A woman he'd once known briefly had called it a defense mechanism. She'd been into pop psychology and thought she had his number.

Defense mechanism? No way. He simply liked his life just fine the way it was, and saw no reason to change it. And dammit, he was *not* lonely, no matter what anyone said! Anytime he wanted company, all he had to do was pick up the phone. Could a man have it any better than that? All the fun, none of the hassles?

There was a row of broken shells on the kitchen windowsill and he wondered if that was a clue to the kind of woman Stu had married. Was there some hidden psychological meaning here? What sort of person would bring home broken shells? Judging solely from the wedding photos, the bride could be a model or a starlet. She had the looks. According to Stu, she was supposed to be working on a degree in linguistics.

What the hell was linguistics, anyway?

A long-haired yellow cat with a wide head and ragged ears stalked into the kitchen and glared at him. Rafe glared back. "Don't even think about it, friend," he growled, plopping the turkey into the sink.

"*Balderdash!*" screamed one of the two African Grays from the living room.

"Yeah, right," Rafe grumbled as he ran water through the cavity and wondered if he'd remembered to buy prepared stuffing. He was getting a low-pressure headache. Either that, or second thoughts were piling in faster than his brain could process them.

The second parrot tuned up with a creditable imitation of a squeaking door, followed by a realistic smoker's hack. From there, things went rapidly downhill.

Rafe wanted to get dinner in the oven before he started checking around for a hotel room. At least since his first disastrous attempt to create a Thanksgiving feast for a desolate kid, he'd learned to remove the unmentionables inside the bird before cramming in the store-bought stuffing.

"Help! Lemme go! Bad-ass, bad-ass!"

"Shut up, you red-tailed devil, or you're going into the oven with baldie here."

If Stu's lovely linguist bride was responsible for her birds' vocabulary, she was a hell of a lot tougher than she looked. Remembering the pictures of the gorgeous vision in white clinging to a beaming Stu reminded Rafe of another reason why he was here instead of being back in Pelican's Cove, Florida, inspecting his latest acquisition to get some idea of how much was salvageable.

Belle was getting married this weekend. Long-legged, sexy Belle, his mistress of the past eight months, who was every bit as good in bed as she was on the tennis courts. They'd met at a yacht christening and promptly entered into the relationship with both pairs of eyes wide open. Rafe had made a point of sharing his philosophy right up front. Except for the five years when Stu lived with him, his motto had always been easy come, easy go. Work hard, play hard, and avoid encumbrances. If he lost everything today, he'd start over tomorrow. Once he'd launched his kid brother and gotten his own life back on track, he had quickly reverted to his old lifestyle. Life was an adventure, he remembered telling Belle at some point. He made a point of not setting up any false expectations. While he was scrupulously faithful to one woman at a time, the last thing he wanted was an anchor holding him down. When the time came to move on, he simply moved on. When both sides clearly understood the ground rules, moving on was easy.

Both he and Belle were in their late thirties and unencumbered. Rafe had been wildly attracted to her body and Belle had been equally attracted to the life-style of a young, moderately wealthy bachelor. Rafe prided himself on being a generous lover, both phys-ically and financially. And he had been, right up until Belle's biological alarm clock had gone off. Six weeks after she had regretfully handed him his walk-ing papers in exchange for a gold charm bracelet and a block of stock, she'd snagged herself an insurance salesman. The last time he'd heard from her they were shopping for a house near a good school.

Rafe wished her luck because he'd genuinely liked the woman. But he'd been feeling increasingly rest-less ever since he'd heard the news. He'd had his personal assistant pick out an expensive wedding gift, and then he'd rearranged his calendar and filed a flight plan to an off-the-beaten-track island on North Carolina's Outer Banks.

A mile away, Molly struggled to hide a yawn. They'd spent a few hours driving along the beach, and for a little while she'd felt like the heroine of one of those adventure movies, racing along the beach, splashing through the surf with the wind blowing in her face and an attractive man at her side.

Jeffy liked open windows. Said he could smell a school of fish a mile out at sea. Over the roar of the wind, he had told her about his father's concrete block business and his own high school football career, and the trophy-size channel bass he'd taken a few years ago. He had perfect teeth, Molly noted absently during the monologue, and a really nice smile. Actually, he was good company if she overlooked a few minor detractions. His jokes were a little raw, but then, the new Molly wasn't going to be as big a prude as the old Molly had been.

After driving from one end of the island to the other, Jeffy insisted on stopping off for a seafood dinner at Delroy's Pub. By that time she was too hungry to resist. Which meant she was going to have to starve for days to make up for the fried scallops and French fries, even though she had left one of each on her plate.

And then someone fed the jukebox. As soon as the music started, two couples got up to dance. From a corner booth, Molly watched, tapping time on the tabletop.

"Hey, come on, what do you say we show 'em how it's done?" Jeffy stood and held out his hand. There was a chorus of whistles and catcalls from the bar and he turned and bowed, grinning at his buddies.

"I don't—" she started to say, but he cut her off.

"Sure you do, honey. Everybody does. Just do what comes naturally."

What came naturally was to disappear. To hole up in her room with a book. But that was the old Molly, and she had sworn that once she left West Virginia she was going to reinvent herself.

The music was loud and fast. Even those who weren't dancing were swaying and tapping their feet. It was a convivial group, just as Sally Ann had said. Ready for a good time. Beer was served by the pitcher and everything on the seafood platter was fried. And so far, Molly had enjoyed everything except the beer.

But dancing? "I'm not very good at this," she protested breathlessly while Jeffy twisted and snapped his fingers. She wasn't dressed for it, either. Some women weren't built for snug jeans and T-shirts. She was getting there, but she still had a long way to go.

"Just shake it, honey. That's all you have to do."

She slid out of the booth and tried her best to "shake it" without actually *shaking* it. The music was mostly beat with no discernible melody, but the rhythm was contagious. She was actually beginning to enjoy herself when one of the men at the bar yelled, "Hey, Jeffy, what happened to that gold ring you usually wear?"

Without answering, Jeffy managed to twist around until he was between her and the men at the bar. "Ignore 'em. They're drunk."

They weren't drunk, but neither were they sober. She asked breathlessly, "What ring is he talking about? Did you lose one at the beach?"

"I never wear a ring when I'm fishing."

And then, just like that, it hit her. It was written all over those bedroom eyes of his. Guilt. She should have recognized it, having seen so much of it in the past. "What ring? Jeffy, are you married?"

"Aw, c'mon, honey, do I look married?"

"Not to me, you don't," she said, and he could

take that any way he wanted to. She headed for the table, where she'd left her damp, sandy embroidered denim jacket and her shoulder bag. She would pay for her own darned supper. She was going to be paying for it in other ways, she might as well go all the way.

"Come on, Moll, be a sport." She dug into her bag and came up with her wallet.

Jeffy shook his head. "No way—put your money back. When a gentleman invites a lady out to supper, she don't have to pay her way."

"Then thank you."

"Aw, come on, sugar, be a sport." He was whining. If there was one thing she hated in a man, it was whining.

"You could have told me." She headed toward the door, with Jeffy right on her heels. People were staring, some of them grinning, a few calling out comments.

"You tell him, sugar!"

"Go get 'er, tiger!"

Feeling her face burning, Molly was glad for the dim lights.

"I was going to tell you, honest. See, me and Shirl, we been having a little trouble and I figured on getting to know you better and then maybe asking how you'd handle it if you was me. I mean, a woman like you, I could tell right off you were the understanding type."

"No you couldn't, because I'm not," Molly said flatly. She had done all the understanding she intended to do, and it had gotten her nowhere. She might be a slow learner, but eventually the message got through.

It was dark. The rain was coming down in solid sheets, blowing across the highway. She hesitated, trying to get her bearings, and then Jeffy opened the door of his truck. "I'll drive you home. I owe you that much."

She was tempted to refuse, but even the old Molly had better sense. It was pitch dark and pouring rain. Given her track record she would probably walk right off the edge of the island and drown.

Jeffy drove her home. He was a sullen companion, but then, so was she. She didn't know whom she was angrier with, Jeffy or herself. She should never have gotten into the truck in the first place. So she'd met him once before on the ferry—he was still a stranger. He'd seemed friendly and likable, but he was a man— a married man. She couldn't afford another of those in her life. Her bank balance hadn't recovered from the last one.

His fishing buddies had stood at the bar all evening, drinking beer, laughing, talking. It hadn't struck her at the time, but not once had any of them come over to the table to be introduced. That had to mean something…didn't it?

Feeling more miserable by the minute, Molly wondered if he had done the whole thing on a dare. *Five bucks says you won't pick up the fat girl. Ten says you won't show up with her at Delroy's.* It wouldn't be the first time she'd been the butt of a joke.

She wasn't all that fat, she thought defensively. She had measurements. She might use up a few more inches on the measuring tape than some other women but she had a shape.

Jeff double-parked outside the cottage, blocking the street. The yard light was on, and for the life of her, she couldn't recall if it was automatic or not. There was a beach buggy wedged in next to her own ten-year-old sedan, the two vehicles squeezed between a picket fence and a massive live oak tree. Sally Ann had warned her that parking was a haphazard affair at best, and once the season got underway, it was next to impossible.

"Thank you for supper and bringing me home," she muttered, all in one breath.

"Hey, Moll, I'm sorry. Really."

"Why me?" There was obviously something about her that attracted lying, conniving losers.

"'Cause you're nice? 'Cause you looked sort of lonesome on the ferry, and I just decided, what the hell? You know how it is."

"No, not really."

"Most women—you know, like they expect a man to blow his paycheck on 'em, and then they cut him dead if he wants a little fun."

"And you wanted a little fun, right?" Sally Ann had warned her about that, too, but she hadn't listened.

"If it had worked out that way." He shrugged. "I wish now I'd told you about Shirl—my wife. Like I said, we're having some problems. She wanted me to skip the tournament just so I could go to this reunion thing, and we sorta had us some words before I left. You're a real good listener. You prob'ly could've given me some tips on how to handle situations like that."

Oh, yes, she was a grand listener. She had listened to a description of every fish the man had caught in last year's tournament, legal or otherwise, including the weight and length, and what type of tackle he had used. She had listened three times to the description of his game-winning touchdown against Marcus P. Struthers High in the regional play-offs.

Just as she had listened to another man explaining earnestly why he could never hold a job, or why he needed to dress for success, and what he was going to do for her once his ship came in.

Kenny's ship had never left harbor. The last thing she needed was a man whose only ship was a smelly old ferryboat. And what's more, she didn't care if he never caught another fish in his entire life, she was tired of trying to solve problems for men who didn't have the gumption to solve their own.

''Thanks again for supper.'' She opened her door and dropped to the ground before he could come around and help her out, not that he made a move to get out of the vehicle. It was raining hard, after all. Head down, she jogged up the path to the cottage, stomped the sand from her feet on the front porch and opened the door.

The kitchen light was on. It had been midafternoon when she'd left, so she wouldn't have turned on any light except for the one by the birdcages. Molly swallowed hard, clutching the plastic bag that held her apples and the broken shells she'd collected earlier. Could Stu and Anna have come home early? Could she have made a mistake and barged into the wrong house?

Hardly. Not with those familiar raucous cries coming from the living room. Not with that smelly long-haired cat wreathing her ankles. She'd gotten lost more than once before she'd found her way around the village, using the map on the tourist brochure, but not this time. This was definitely the right house.

Cautiously she moved inside and peered into the kitchen. The bag fell from her fingers. Apples rolled across the sloping floor. She stared openmouthed at the tall, tanned and sun-streaked guy with a dish towel tucked into his belt and a dead turkey cradled in his arms.

Rafe, on hearing a car door slam outside, had peered out the window to see a woman jump down from a dark green pickup truck and hurry up the path to the front porch. He waited for Stu to join her, but the truck drove off.

But then, Stu didn't drive a truck. He drove an expensive toy his father had given him for his twenty-first birthday to make up for a lifetime of neglect.

It also occurred to Rafe that unless the wedding photographer had used a trick lens, this was definitely not the bride.

Rafe was still standing there with the bird all ready for the oven when the woman appeared in the kitchen doorway. Neither of them spoke for a moment. ''Surprise, congratulations and happy birthday, kid,'' didn't seem appropriate.

No way was this Stu's bride. Somebody had a lot of explaining to do. Even wearing wet denim instead of white satin, there was no resemblance. Stu's bride was a tall, slender beauty. This woman was none of the above.

Housekeeper? Housebreaker? Mother-in-law? Friend of the family? ''You want to go first?'' he offered.

''I think you'd better go first, starting with what you're doing in my kitchen.'' Her voice was the most striking thing about her. Husky, but with a hint of firmness that was unmistakable.

"*Your* kitchen?"

"I asked who you are," she reminded him with a take-no-hostages glint in her whiskey-colored eyes.

"Actually you didn't, but I'll tell you anyway. Name's Rafe Webber. And if this is your kitchen, then you must be—?" He was momentarily distracted by seeing her eyes narrow. Eyes that big and slumberous weren't equipped to look suspicious, but she managed it anyway.

"Rafe Webber? Is that supposed to ring a bell?"

Well, hell... He wasn't used to having to explain himself. He'd long since earned the privilege of asking the questions, not having to answer them. "You have the advantage of me, Miss—?" A gentleman to the bitter end, he thought with wry amusement. His headache wasn't getting any better.

"Until I know what you're doing here, I don't have to tell you anything. How did you get in?"

"Front door. It wasn't locked. I figured Stu would be back any minute."

"You know Stu?"

He decided to cut her some slack. Had a feeling it might save time and trouble in the long run. "He's my brother."

"Stu's name isn't Webber. Try again."

The lady was sharp. In no mood to go into the convoluted relationships in his immediate family, Rafe kept it simple. "We're half brothers. Same mother, different fathers."

"Do you have some identification?"

Deep breath. Open oven door, insert turkey, shut door and smile. Turning back, he said, "Dammit, lady, I don't need any identification, I know who I am. And I know you're not Stu's wife, so suppose you produce some identification of your own.''

In clinging wet jeans and a baggy wet jacket it was obvious that she was carrying a few extra pounds. For reasons he didn't even try to dissect, a few of his defenses crumbled. The place wasn't big enough for a full-scale war. It was your bottom-line basic seventy-year-old cottage, with slightly newer appliances. He thought about the wedding gift he'd had shipped to Stu's apartment in Durham, a fancy piece of equipment that did everything from poaching salmon to pouring tea, or so he'd been told by the salesman. With it he'd ordered monthly shipments of salmon and prime beef. God knew where they were now. Rotting in some post office, probably.

The woman stared pointedly at the towel around his waist until he whipped it off and flung it at the counter. It fell to the floor. In the next room, the parrots cut loose with a stream of profanities, which didn't help matters.

''They're next, as soon as I get another pan ready.'' He nodded to the oven.

Her eyes widened without losing the look of suspicion. She glanced down at the apples on the floor as if wondering how they'd got there. Glanced at him as if wondering the same thing.

Rafe had to admit the kitchen was a mess. When it came to cooking he was used to state-of-the-art equipment and someone to clean up after him. He said, ''You're wet.''

Without breaking eye contact, she said in that firm, husky voice, ''It's raining.''

So what now? he wondered. He scooped her apple bag off the floor and discovered it was half full of shells. Sandy, broken shells. At least one mystery had been cleared up, which left only a dozen or so to go.

She slipped off her wet jacket and hung it on a hook by the back door. Rafe let his eyes do the walking. The term Rubenesque came to mind. As for her face, it was…interesting. At the moment she looked as if a smile would fracture her jaw, but her skin was the kind a woman had to be born with. Cosmetics could never achieve that buttery smooth texture. He'd seen too many women come to regret having spent half their lives sunbathing not to recognize the difference.

"I don't suppose you know where they are?" He decided on a flank attack. She still hadn't told him who she was, but that could wait. Once the honeymooners got home, they could do the honors.

"Who, Annamarie and Stu?" The look of suspicion was replaced by a look of puzzlement. Or maybe she was just nearsighted. "They're supposed to be in Jamestown."

"Jamestown," he repeated. And then "*Jamestown?* As in Virginia? What the hell are they doing there? I'm cooking their supper."

"Um…studying the diggings. I guess."

"Studying the diggings. You want to run that by me again?"

"It's Annamarie's birthday present."

He shook his head. "Somebody gave her a trip to Jamestown for a birthday gift?" A change in barometric pressure always did a number on his head. This time it had evidently affected his hearing, as well.

With a majestic sigh, the woman said, "It's Annamarie's gift to Stu. He's the historian, as you should know if you really are who you say you are. While they're down here working on her thesis, she's giving him this side trip for a birthday present.''

Rafe pressed his cool fingertips above his eyes and rubbed. With a sigh, he said, ''Look, Miss—''

''Dewhurst. And it's Ms., not Miss. Annamarie is my baby sister.''

''Ms. Dewhurst,'' he repeated. Great. He'd come all this way, planning to check out his new half sister-in-law and make up to Stu for all the missed occasions with a belated birthday feast, and now he was stuck here with Ms. Congeniality.

''Actually, it's Molly,'' she said in that quiet, husky voice of hers that kept getting between him and his anger.

Make that frustration. ''Well, Molly, whoever you are and whatever you're doing here, I hope you like turkey. And candied sweet potatoes and spoon bread and whatever green vegetable I can find in Stu's pantry. It'll probably be canned peas, but with enough butter and seasoning, they're not half bad.''

''Balderdash, balderdash, balderda—!''

Moving swiftly, Rafe closed the door between the two rooms, making the kitchen seem smaller than ever. The whole cottage would fit nicely into his suite at his latest acquisition, a small resort hotel on Florida's Gulf Coast.

''I think we'd better talk,'' Ms. Molly Dewhurst said as she shucked off a pair of very wet pink sneakers. ''But first I really need a cup of coffee. It might be April, but I'm freezing.'' As if to prove her point, she sneezed, begged his pardon and said, ''You're welcome to a cup if you don't mind reheated.''

Three

The coffee was weak and decaffeinated, but it served to wash down a couple of aspirin. "Okay, so talk." His company manners were fading fast.

"Talk. All right. What if I pay you for the groceries and you catch the next ferry out?"

He didn't bother to tell her he'd flown in, and until the weather broke, he wouldn't be flying out again. "I've got a better idea," he countered. "What if you catch the ferry and I stay here and house-sit until the happy couple gets back?"

Slowly Molly shook her head. A few more lengths of damp brown hair worked free to brush her shoulders. Dry and left to its own devices, it would probably pass as a crowning glory. Thick, red highlights and a tendency to curl.

"What was that?" Distracted, he'd missed her reply.

"I said I'm not going anywhere. I promised Annamarie I'd stay here and look after Shag and the birds, and I always keep my promises."

"Always?"

"Practically always."

"Then you're one woman in a million."

"I don't know what to say to that, but I'll tell you this much—I'm staying. So if you want to hang around until they get back, I hope you've secured a room. I know it's early in the season, but with this tournament thing and all, they're probably pretty full."

Rafe never knew what made him dig in his heels. It sure as the devil wasn't the woman's personal attractions. She was a frump with pretty hair, a sexy voice, nice eyes and great skin. Period. "I've got a better idea. Why don't *you* book a room?"

"Because I can't afford it," she said flatly. The last thing he was prepared for was a straight answer. Unless she was angling for a pay-off. "And because I promised I'd take care of things. I've never met you before, never even heard of you. That is, I knew Stu had a brother who didn't bother to show up for the wedding, but for all I know, you could be just another—another beach bum, looking for a place to stay."

Rafe tipped his chair back and closed his eyes. When he opened them again, she was still there. Obdurate. Yeah, that was a good description. "What if I pay the tab? Would you go then?"

Huffy. Another good description.

"I beg your pardon," she said loftily.

He had to laugh. Headache and all. "Well, of course you do, honey. What about, How dare you?

Want to run that one by me while you're dishing up indignation?'' And then he relented. ''Look, you don't trust me and I don't particularly trust you.'' Actually he was almost beginning to, which came as something of a surprise. ''So what do you say we strike a bargain? I'll check out the room situation, but if I can't find a vacancy, I'll bed down in the room with the miserable-looking cot buried under all the junk, and you can have the queen-size bed with a view of the cemetery.''

''Oh, but—''

''I'll do the cooking, you look after the birds, we'll both watch to see that nobody steals the family silver, and if the honeymooners aren't back by the time the weather breaks, I'll leave.'' He might. He might not. ''Fair enough? Meanwhile I'll do my best to stay out of your hair.''

Which was beginning to curl around her face. Half the women he knew had gone red this year. He'd lay odds she was the genuine article. Even her eyebrows were auburn.

Outside, the rain pounded down harder than ever. The trouble with Hatteras Lows was that they had a tendency to hang around too long, flooding highways, cutting new inlets, generally messing things up.

''Well, I guess… I mean, all right, we'll give it a try. But I'm warning you, if I find out you're not who you say you are—''

Rafe taught the parrots a new word. ''Look, can you think of another reason why any man in his right mind would show up on Ocracoke Island in this kind of weather when he could be down in sunny Florida sharing a pitcher of margaritas with a pretty woman and watching preseason baseball?''

* * *

The truce lasted until dinner was served. Molly had already eaten dinner, but that had been hours ago. Since then she had burned up a lot of emotional energy. She had spent the last few hours trying to ignore the tempting smells permeating the whole house while she shifted stacks of books, tapes and taping equipment off the cot and spread it with clean, if musty-smelling, sheets. After that she'd spent an hour or so trying to concentrate on the paperback novel she'd brought to read on the beach while the stranger in her kitchen slammed pots and pans together and muttered under his breath.

He might or might not be Stu's brother. Men lied. Besides, they didn't look anything at all alike. Stu had freckles, red-blond hair that fell over his forehead and a jack-o'-lantern grin. He claimed to have three sisters and one brother, but none of them had showed up at the wedding. His mother was supposed to be somewhere in Europe, and he wasn't quite sure where his father was. According to Annamarie, they weren't at all close.

As for the volunteer chef, he looked like an advertisement for some tropical resort. Tall, tanned, with sun-bleached hair and a pair of pale gray eyes that were clear as rainwater yet impossible to read. Like a trick mirror. His features were far from perfect—his nose a tad too large, his jaw a bit too strong. His cheekbones were more flat and angular than high and aristocratic.

All of which made it hard to understand why she suddenly found herself redefining everything she had ever considered physically attractive in a man. If she needed to prove how wretched her judgment was when it came to men, she had two perfect examples to refer to. Smooth-talking Kenny and Stallone-look-alike Jeffy. Even their names sounded immature.

Their *names* sounded immature? Oh, for heaven's sake, it must be the weather. On a rainy night like this, with nothing to distract her, her mind obviously had a mind of its own.

"Blue cheese okay?"

Molly glanced up at the man in the doorway and caught her breath all over again. Telling herself to quit staring, she managed to say, "Blue's fine."

Any kind of cheese was fine, since she wouldn't be indulging. She had a feeling she could gain weight just looking at that delectable mouth of his and wondering...

Wondering nothing. All she needed to know was what he was doing here, why he was going to all this trouble and how long he intended to stay. At the rate it was raining, the roads would soon be flooded. Sally Ann had mentioned something about high water tables and creeks backing up. If it got much worse, not even the ferries would run, which meant they would be trapped here together.

What if he was lying about being Stu's brother? Men always lied when it was to their advantage. Her ex-husband was a prime example. As her neighbor back in Grover's Hollow had said when she learned that Molly was planning to marry Kenneth Dewhurst, "You don't want to do that, honey. He talks real pretty but there ain't a speck o' truth in him."

Jeffy of the beer cans and bedroom eyes had lied, at least by omission. This man could be lying, too, but for the life of her she couldn't think of a single reason why he should. There was no reason for him to stay, as Stu wouldn't be back for several days. Let him head on back to Florida and his margaritas and pretty women.

With a restless sigh, she laid her book aside. Her stomach growled, either in protest of the fried food she had consumed earlier or anticipation from the delectable smells issuing from the kitchen. She was accustomed to eating early and going to bed before she succumbed to late-night temptation. Not even to herself would she admit that tonight's temptation might involve more than food.

She wandered over to the birdcages and checked the water cups. There was a grape in one. "Messy, aren't you? I'll take care of it tomorrow. It's your bedtime now."

As usual, her comments were greeted by a cacophony of gutter language and filthy suggestions, "*Stick it up yer arse*" being one of the milder ones.

"Eat soap and die," she growled as she snatched her fingers from the danger zone.

"*Bill-ee, shaddup! Bill-ee, shaddup!*"

"Both of you shut up, or I'll—"

"*Balderdash. Hell-oo, honey!*"

"Don't you honey me, you dirty old man." Their names were Pete and Repete. A little too cute, but then, they were Annamarie's problem, not hers.

Pete—or maybe it was the other one—did a flushing toilet and then a series of noises that reminded her of someone cracking his knuckles. Molly ignored it and reached for the sheets to cover the cages.

"*Belly up, down the hatch, belly up, down the hatch!*"

"Just hush up and go to sleep." Her stomach growled once more as she picked up her book and settled down in the slipcovered easy chair again. It was a grisly murder-mystery, the last thing she needed on a night like this with a stranger in the house.

And she was hungry again. It wasn't fair. Both her sisters, Annamarie and Mary, took after the Stevenses, who were all tall and lean and burned up calories without even trying. Molly had taken after her mother's family. The fact that hips and thighs were supposed to be the healthiest place to store fat didn't help. She'd rather not have to store it at all.

It was almost eleven. Normally she would have eaten a light supper at six and been in bed by now. Shag, the half-Persian, half-coon cat Annamarie had had for years, climbed onto her lap, circled and settled down. He smelled like fish. She'd been buying him special treats at the fish market so that he wouldn't wander away and get lost and break Annamarie's heart.

"Dinner is served, madam. I thought a nice merlot. Okay with you?"

She didn't even know what a merlot was, only that it was a wine, and if she had to use up her daily allotment of calories, she intended to use it on something she liked a lot better than she did wine. "Um...water will be fine."

The kitchen table had been spread with a sheet. There was no dining room. No table linens, either. But there were hurricane candles, and her genial host—a little too genial to be trusted—had stuck them into a pair of red glass holders he'd found somewhere and used them as a centerpiece. There wasn't room on the table for the turkey.

"Oh, no, not candied yams." She uttered a soft moan.

"Butter, coconut, orange juice, pecans and brown sugar. Here, try some." He'd cooked enough to feed a platoon.

"Just a taste," she said, not wanting to hurt his feelings. "I ate earlier." Darn it, she'd come so close to having cheekbones. She had lost weight during the breakup of her marriage, but after Kenny had followed her to her next job and made such a pest of himself that they'd found an excuse to let her go, she had nibbled the pounds back again.

Poor Kenny. It wasn't that he was stupid, because he really wasn't. The trouble was, he worked so hard trying to keep from working that he never got anywhere. It hadn't taken long after they were married to discover that he had fallen for her earning capacity, not her looks or her personality. For years she had worked two jobs to put her sisters through college. By the time she'd met Kenny, she was well on the way to rebuilding her savings account, with every intention of cultivating a whole new Molly Stevens, minus the extra pounds and plus a whole lot more pizzazz.

Just as she was ready to reach out for something of her own, Kenny Dewhurst had appeared on the scene. He'd been briefly employed as a sales rep for a farm implement company at the time, despite the fact that he knew little or nothing about farming. But in a tiny place like Grover's Hollow, he'd created something of a sensation. All the girls were talking about him, but to everyone's astonishment, it was Molly he'd singled out. Smooth, handsome—short for a man, but just right for her—he had called her darling. Not honey, or babe, but darling. She'd been in awe of this man who spent more on one pair of shoes than she spent on her entire best outfit, and he drove a convertible, besides.

The convertible had been repossessed two weeks after their wedding because Kenny had had a falling-out with his boss, quit his job and couldn't make the payments. By that time he was no longer calling her darling, or even honey. His famous-name shoes had lasted a lot longer than his charm, but by then she wouldn't have cared if he wore golden slippers. Her neighbor had been right. Not only was he a world-class liar, he hadn't a grain of ambition. Two jobs were enough for any married couple, and she had both of them.

Besides, he was working on "something big." Kenny was always "working on something big." She hadn't dared quit her home-bookkeeping business because her job at the bank, while the title was nice, didn't pay a whole lot. Meanwhile, Kenny went right on working on his Big Deal. So far as Molly was concerned, his Big Deal was making such a pest of himself that he'd managed to get her fired from the bank, and later on, from a job with a small insurance company before they'd separated. She'd left her next job voluntarily after a break-in, because she suspected him of having something to do with it.

Not that she'd ever voiced her suspicions, either to Kenny or the authorities, because the divorce had come through by then, and the last thing she wanted was another kind of involvement with her ex. She had given him every chance to live up to his promises, but he never had. She had tried to understand his point of view—that he was slated for better things, that he'd had some bad breaks, that nobody understood him. It all boiled down to one thing. Besides being bone lazy, Kenny Dewhurst lacked so much as a grain of integrity. He was a failure. He would always be a failure because he refused to listen to advice or accept help, other than the financial help he demanded.

That was when she'd moved from West Virginia to North Carolina and taken a position as head housekeeper for a small assisted-living home. Two months ago she heard from a friend back in West Virginia that Kenny had been asking about her. That was the main reason she'd jumped at the chance to house-sit for Stu and Annamarie while Holly Hills Home was closed down for renovations. She knew Kenny. He was tenacious as flypaper when he wanted something, but like a child, he was easily distracted. With any luck, he would soon get discouraged and look for some other poor woman to hit on.

"Earth to Ms. Dewhurst."

Molly glanced up at the man seated across the table and was struck all over again by the combination of rugged features, pale gray eyes and a crooked grin. So he was attractive. Okay, so he was devastatingly attractive. For a woman who had any number of marketable skills, she was notoriously bad when it came to judging character, but at least knowing her weakness, she was forewarned.

"More spoon bread?"

"What? Oh, no thanks, I never eat—" Oh, my mercy. He had loaded her plate and she'd cleaned it off without even realizing what she was doing. Fifty thousand calories, gone to waste. Make that, gone to waist.

There was no earthly reason, Molly told herself that night as she lay in bed listening to the rain, why they couldn't simply ignore each other and go their own way. Once the rain stopped and the roads were clear, Rafe would probably be more than ready to move on. Then she could go on cleaning cages, brushing a shedding, long-hair cat, counting calories and enjoying her first beach vacation. She'd discovered dozens of purple shell fragments on the beach that Sally Ann told her were bits of ancient clam shells. Remembering a book that had come out a few years ago, about older women wearing purple, she decided to take everyone at the home a handful of purple shell fragments.

A few hours later in another part of the house, Rafe moved restlessly from window to window, looking for a way out. So much for his great instincts and impeccable sense of timing. The least he could have done was to call before he'd gotten himself trapped in an impossible situation.

He switched on the kitchen radio, hoping for news or a weather forecast. He got static. Lightning noise. There was no TV, and even if there were, chances were it wouldn't work any better than the radio. Which meant he was trapped here until the weather cleared. Trapped with a wary female who had a sharp tongue, lambent eyes and the kind of body that would have made her the toast of the town a hundred years ago.

The birds were asleep—at least, their cages were covered. His headache had backed off, but he'd given up trying to sleep. Restless, he located the phone book and settled down with the old black rotary phone to call every damned hotel on the island. Only, instead of a dial tone, he got a sound like a drunk gargling whiskey.

Wet lines. The whole damned island was drowning.

Little Miss Muffet was probably in there snoring her head off. Dammit, if she weren't here to complicate things, he could have at least had himself a busman's holiday. He currently owned two coastal resorts, one recently renovated and reopened, the other in process of being evaluated. He owned a three-boat charter fleet. A day or two of scoping out the local facilities and the whole trip would be a tax write-off.

Not that he begrudged the cost, but he hated like the devil being made to feel like a fool. And now, whichever way he went, it would be wrong. He could hang around for a day or so and find out what needed doing about the woman Stu had married. Or he could take Molly Muffet at her word and leave her to look after those blasphemous birds, trusting to luck that Stu hadn't made the mistake of his life.

Either way, he was pinned down for the time being, and being pinned down wasn't something he bore up under gracefully.

Four

Rafe served Molly, then helped himself to a filet of trout that had been broiled to perfection. The small refrigerator was filled with turkey leftovers. At this rate he'd have to open up a soup kitchen. Until last night his cooking had consisted of the occasional intimate dinner for two, followed by an equally intimate breakfast. This was neither.

"I don't remember seeing you in any of the wedding pictures." It was a harmless observation, but Molly sensed both irritation and frustration.

She glanced up from her plate. "Hmm? Oh, I was somewhere around. I was the one in blue." Navy blue. Because dark colors were slenderizing. She had hoped to be able to fit into something more festive in time for Annamarie's wedding, but thanks to another unpleasant surprise visit from her ex, she had nibbled herself out of that possibility.

One of three Stevens sisters growing up back in West Virginia, Molly had been called the plump one to distinguish her from the gorgeous one and the brainy one. The brainy one was now an assistant research chemist in St. Louis, and the beauty was currently in Jamestown, exploring the excavations with her new husband.

"How's the fish?"

"Delicious." At least broiled fish was something she could enjoy with a clear conscience. She'd even eaten half a baked potato with salt and pepper only.

"Getting it fresh makes the difference. Squirt on the lemon juice, pour on the melted butter and bingo! You've got yourself a real treat."

"Butter?"

"Don't even think about using margarine." Rafe helped himself to the other half of her baked potato and ladled on the sour cream.

She sighed. "All right, I won't."

He looked at her, a frown shadowing his eyes. "Hey, you're not worried about a little butter, are you? Dairy foods are one of the major food groups."

Shag, the cat, shoved his head against her leg, reminding her that he, too, enjoyed seafood, with or without condiments. "Look, it's not a problem, all right? You go on cooking the things you like to cook, and I'll go on eating the things I want to eat. Better yet, you move out and I'll manage on my own."

"Not an option. Unfortunately."

"Unfortunately," she echoed under her breath.

"You don't eat enough," he said, still with that look of fake concern on his winter-tanned face. And that was another thing Molly hated about men. Hypocrisy. Kenny had been so worried about her when she'd had the flu. Worried about her losing her day job and falling behind on her home bookkeeping business.

Molly carefully folded her napkin and shoved her chair back. "If you'll excuse me, I need to go clean cages. Put away the food and I'll take care of the dishes." The cottage didn't run to a dishwasher, which had been just fine when all she'd had to clean up after were her own simple meals. With Rafe the Wonder Chef doing the honors, it was something else again.

"I made double chocolate parfait for dessert." He gave her a sly look that made her want to grind his baked potato, sour cream and all, into his crooked grin.

Closing her eyes, she prayed for patience, or at least a metabolism that wasn't so laid-back she could gain weight from reading a recipe. "Did you have to do that?" she asked plaintively.

"I could've made key lime pie," he said, all innocence, "but I didn't have the ingredients. I only know three desserts."

And so it went for the next few days while the low hung on, bringing gale force winds and torrential rains. For reasons Molly couldn't begin to fathom, Rafe tried to win her over with calories, while she tried her best to resist. To resist both his irresistible kitchen skills and his unmistakable charm.

Because charming he was, even discounting the attraction of his mismatched features. Molly could have sworn she was immune to all forms of masculine charm, but she'd never been exposed to Rafe Webber. Jeffy the jerk had been obvious once she'd come to her senses. At first she'd been flattered, and then she'd thought, where was the harm in a little friendly flirting? Wasn't a flirtation supposed to be included in any dream vacation package?

But once the novelty wore off, she hadn't liked what she'd seen. An unfaithful husband who whined. So far as she knew, Kenny had never been truly unfaithful to her, for all his other faults. Probably because he loved himself far more than he could ever love any woman. But his whining had been the last of a whole haystack full of last straws.

And now, just when she was beginning to regain her self-confidence, she found herself weathered in with a stealth charmer like Rafe Webber. That thick, sun-streaked hair and the sheer physical presence were striking, but the crooked nose, the crooked smile and the juggernaut jaw should have minimized the effect. Instead, it did just the opposite. Either she was allergic or he was addictive. Now she knew how it felt to be a scrap of iron, with a powerful magnet close by.

Not again, no thank you, no way! She'd traveled that route before. Once her sisters were launched and on the way to paying off the last of the loans, she had reached into life's grab bag for something of her own and come up with a handsome, charming scoundrel. The fact that she'd actually married him just went to show that where men were concerned, she hadn't a clue.

Maybe she should try wearing blinders, like the brick maker's pug mill mule back in Grover's Hollow. She had a feeling, though, that blinders wouldn't help with a man like Rafe Webber. She could cover her head with a pillowcase and still know if he was anywhere near.

"What do you do for entertainment?" he asked as he poured two cups of coffee and handed her one.

"If this rain doesn't end, I might take up boating, only I don't have a boat."

"How about shipbuilding? We might need an ark if it gets much deeper. Did you say this was your first trip to the beach, or did I only imagine it?"

"I probably said it." She said all sorts of things when she was ill at ease, as if running her mouth could forestall facing up to whatever trouble she'd blundered into. "I've got all sorts of plans for when the rain stops and the water goes down."

"Surfing? Kayaking?"

"Um…there's a museum."

"Wreck diving? Sunbathing?" He raised one eyebrow in a way that put her instantly on the defensive.

"I don't know how to dive. I don't even know how to swim. As for sunbathing, in case you hadn't noticed, it's cold, windy and raining." As if she would bare her body in public, on even the sunniest day. After Kenny's first cutting remarks about her figure, she'd cried herself sick and then demolished three-quarters of a coconut cream pie.

"I'm going to make a supply run. Want to go with me, or—"

"I'd better cut up more vegetables for the birds."

She watched him through the window, hatless, but wearing a waterproof slicker. With any luck he'd grow tired of waiting and go back to Florida's high-rent district, where he'd picked up that devastating suntan and the kind of casual sophistication Kenny had tried so hard to imitate. She didn't know which was worse—the imitation or the real thing.

Yes, she did. Imitations were like cheap toys—showy, but quickly broken.

She was beginning to believe the real thing could tempt her in ways she could barely imagine.

"Hey, bitch, wanna grape?"

"Hush up, you foul-mouthed creature," she muttered, viciously chopping carrots into manageable slivers. Raw vegetables didn't tempt her at all. Unfortunately.

After that she marched into the living room and carefully pulled the tray out from the bottom of the cage. Food, feathers and droppings clumped together in the orange litter. "Messy birds," she scolded. They had to be male. Her sisters had been well trained to look after themselves, but she had never known a man, including her own father, who didn't expect a woman to clean up after them.

"Shaddup, shaddup, shaddup!"

And then Pete tuned up with his favorite litany of four-letter words, which Molly did her best to ignore. Once both cages were cleaned and all cups washed and refilled, she stared out the window at the rain and sighed. What now? Wash the dishes, make her bed and then settle down with a boring murder-mystery? One thing she wasn't about to do was stay here alone, with the refrigerator crammed full of temptation. She'd given her powers of resistance a workout these past few days.

Besides, she'd promised Annamarie to check the mailbox every few days to clear out the junk mail. That meant a walk to the post office, as there was no house delivery on the island.

She bundled up in her tan raincoat and pulled a matching hat on her head. Both items had long since lost most of their protective qualities, but an umbrella, even if she'd brought one with her, wouldn't stand a chance in this wind. What she needed was one of those cheap plastic raincoats. Something in a bold color, maybe orange or yellow or neon green.

The roads were flooded. Cars got through by driving slowly and throwing up a big wake. Molly didn't even want to think about what might be lurking under all that murky water. She'd borrowed a pair of Stu's rubber boots, which were several inches too long for her feet but high enough to protect her from whatever yucky creatures swam in the floodwaters. If she'd had a grain of common sense, she would have taken Rafe up on his offer, but she couldn't afford any more of his brand of temptation.

Imagine waffles for breakfast. Served with butter and homemade fig preserves. She could hardly decline without hurting his feelings after he'd gone to so much trouble, but she was going to have to slog three times around the island in knee-deep water to work off all the calories.

From now on, she vowed, her rare indulgences would not include food. A woman needed to feel good about herself, and to do that she had to know she looked her best. Straining side seams and hollowless cheeks weren't going to help. A sagging, wet tan raincoat might describe the way she looked on the outside, but not the way she felt on the inside. A bright orange raincoat was more what she needed. Orange had attitude. It worked for highway workers. It worked for the Coast Guard. Maybe if she got herself a bright orange slicker it would work for her.

Hey, wake up, world! Here's Molly, in all her glory!

Rafe might think she was dull as ditch water— Kenny had considered her only as a convenient meal ticket and a shoulder to cry on until something better came along, but Molly knew who she was. It might not show on the outside, but the *real* Molly was bold and imaginative.

Well…maybe sensible and capable was a better description. And maybe a pretty shade of blue would be better. She would never be as smart as Mary Etta, whose SAT scores had been highest in the state the year she'd graduated from high school, or as beautiful as Annamarie, who'd been queen of the Apple Festival and voted the prettiest girl at GHHS.

Still, it was Molly who had held the family together after the folks had been killed. Long before that she'd been working and squirreling away her earnings to go off to college. Instead, she had seen that her two sisters, seven and nine years younger, respectively, had a shot at the gold ring. Mary Etta had gone to college on a scholarship but even so, Molly's help had been needed. Now that both sisters were secure and on their own, it was her turn. Without Kenny there was no limit to what she could do.

Rain dripped from her limp hat and trickled down the back of her neck. The last time she'd seen her ex-husband, he had tried to appeal to her better nature, claiming that without her steadying influence, which Molly wisely interpreted to mean her steady income, he would never be able to realize his potential.

"You reached your potential when you were seven years old," she'd told him that day after he'd tracked her down at her office in Morganton to ask if he could move in with her just until he got back on his feet. When she'd refused, he'd sulked until she threatened to call security.

That same night he'd turned up on her doorstep. He'd been drinking, and when she refused to let him inside he'd started crying. So of course she'd had to let him in, and then he'd got sick and ruined the new slipcover she'd bought for her thrift-shop sofa.

Poor Kenny. He was a miserable excuse for a man, but she had done her best and it hadn't helped. What was that old Chinese thing about saving a man's life and being responsible for him from then on?

Evidently it was a universal thing.

It was shortly after that that she'd moved to North Carolina, changing jobs and addresses. She hadn't heard from him since then. With any luck she wouldn't. Because, heaven help her, she thought as she turned off onto Fig Tree Lane, she really did feel sorry for the poor wretch for being such a loser. Nobody, given a choice, would choose to be such a bona fide jerk.

After collecting the mail, Molly considered her options. She could head back to the cottage and settle down with her gory mystery, or wade around the village in the rain, which had slowed to a drizzle. She was still standing outside the post office when the rusty SUV with the bumper bracket full of empty pole holders pulled up. There were countless similar vehicles on the island, but she knew who it was even before Rafe swung open the door. That darned magnetism again.

"Want a lift?"

"No thanks." Without even trying, the man frazzled every cell in her body, up to and including her brain cells. "Just going for a walk."

"Hop in, we'll go to the beach. I need to check up on the Baron anyway."

The baron? What was a baron doing on the Ocracoke beach? Another few synapses shorted out as she stood there and tried to think of a good reason to refuse. Wind whipped her hair across her face. A crew cut. That was next on her makeover after the orange raincoat.

Molly had planned to drive herself to the ocean beach one more time before she left, anyway. Her budget didn't allow for too many pleasure jaunts, because she still had to get herself back home once Annamarie and Stu got back. They hadn't asked about her finances, and she hadn't told them, but right now her bank balance was the skinniest thing about her.

"Come on. Except for a few diehard fishermen, we should have the beach all to ourselves on a day like this." He leaned across the seat and offered her a hand up.

Mentally she added a backbone to her list, right between the raincoat and crew cut. "Thanks," she muttered, squirming on the rump-sprung seat. The inside of the vehicle was almost as wet as the outside. There were rust holes in the floorboard and the window wouldn't quite shut all the way.

"Think of it as another adventure," Rafe said, his weathered face creasing in an infectious grin.

"Adventures are a lot more comfortable between the covers of a book."

"Hey, it's no adventure when all you have to do is close the book and walk away."

"You want alligators snapping at your heels? Help yourself, but count me out."

He chuckled, and somewhat to her surprise, Molly did, too, the sound nearly lost in the noisy roar of a rusted muffler.

Shortly after they left the village behind, Rafe turned onto a paved road that led to an airstrip nestled against the dune line. "Ocracoke International," he announced. "Mind waiting a few minutes? I'll be right back."

Ocracoke International? She'd thought that was the fishing tournament. Or had that been Ocracoke Invitational? Through the intermittent flurries, she counted eight small planes tied down, their cockpits covered with tarps. A flock of low-flying brown pelicans followed the dune line, and Molly marveled that anything could be so ungainly and so beautiful.

Rafe, his yellow slicker incandescent against a slate-gray sky, jogged out onto the tarmac and circled a white plane with a pale green palm tree against an orange sun painted on the side. She watched as he touched this and tugged at that, occasionally nodding. Molly huddled inside the vehicle. No wonder he hadn't been interested in catching a ferry.

"Rain's easing up," he said when he joined her a few minutes later.

"Is that the baron you were referring to?"

He nodded. "Ready to hit the beach?"

She peered through the salt-hazed, sand-pitted windshield. "It doesn't look much like beach weather."

"What, you're afraid of getting wet?" Backing out of the parking space, he shot her a teasing glance that made her acutely aware of her bedraggled appearance.

In the yellow slicker he looked more dashing than ever.

Molly vowed silently to ditch the awful raincoat and hat the minute she got back to the cottage. By then he was on the ramp leading over the dunes. Shifting into neutral, he glanced up and down the windswept beach. Even in the rain it was beautiful. Broad, flat, its white sands a dramatic contrast to the dark, angry water and the steely gray sky. "We'll head north. The rain's about to slack off. By late afternoon we might even catch a glimpse of sunshine." At her look of disbelief, he grinned and said, "What's the matter? Don't you trust me?"

"Not particularly." Trust wasn't that easy for a woman with her track record, but he was right about the rain. By the time he'd driven half a mile or so along the empty shore, it had stopped completely. Molly was too awed by the roiling gray Atlantic to notice until Rafe stopped and pointed it out to her.

"See? When I promise a lady something, I always deliver. Sea's still rough, but the sun's already trying to break through."

As if on command, a shaft of sunlight slanted through the clouds, glinting pale gold on the distant horizon. Molly sighed and leaned forward to peer through the pitted windshield. And then she squeaked, "Oh, my mercy, look at all the shells!"

She was out before he could offer to come around and help her down, never mind that big-wheeled 4x4s had not been designed with short people in mind. Soggy raincoat flapping, she jogged toward the surf in the clumsy boots, where several days of mountainous seas had deposited tons of broken shells.

Rafe joined her there, making a mental note to buy

her some decent rain gear before he left. And a pair of boots that fit. The ones she was wearing looked miles too big. "These are all busted up. There's a whole cockleshell, though. And, hey—here's an unbroken Scotch bonnet."

Molly ignored his perfect finds to pounce on a worn fragment of broken clamshell. "Purple," she crowed. "Did you ever see such a rich color? Oh, and look—there's another one!"

And so it went. Rafe soon discarded his modest finds. Most of the tourist shops along the eastern seaboard had bins filled with perfect shells, all imported. He doubted if anyone had ever expressed as much delight over a queen conch or a perfect murex as Molly did over a few thumbnail-size bits of broken clamshells.

"Oh, look—I know what this is, it's an oyster shell." She slipped a small, nondescript shell into her pocket, which was already bulging with wet, sandy treasures. "It reminds me of a raccoon's foot—the shape and all."

Rafe thought about buying her a shell book so she could identify her finds, but decided against it. No point in spoiling her pleasure. *Bless your little heart, honey. I'd like to turn you loose on my stretch of the coast for a few hours.*

By the time they got back to the cottage, Molly was chilled, even though the temperature had reached the high fifties. She must have walked off at least a pound. That was a down payment on cheekbones...wasn't it?

"We need to warm you up. What'll it be, hot chocolate or Irish coffee?"

"No chocolate, please. I didn't know coffee grew in Ireland, I thought it came from South America."

"Trust me, you'll like it," Rafe said solemnly. If Molly hadn't known better, she might have mistaken the twinkle in his eyes for laughter.

And heaven help her, she did. Loved it! Strong coffee, Irish whiskey, whipped cream and all. "Oh, my mercy, this is delicious," she all but purred. Thank goodness he'd used the teacups instead of the big lighthouse mugs.

One of the troubles with alcohol was that it had too many calories. Another was that it seldom fit into her budget. But worst of all, Molly had learned a long time ago at an office party that when she tippled, she had a tendency to chatter. Since then she had made a conscious effort not to. Not to drink, and not to chatter. "No more, thank you, but it was delicious. Honestly." She manufactured a yawn that turned into the genuine article. "I'm not really much of a drinker."

Sprawled in the room's one easy chair, Rafe studied the woman curled up on the sofa, her feet tucked under her, cheeks flushed from a combination of wind and Bushmill's. She looked about sixteen years old. "Tell me about my new in-laws," he prompted. "There's you, Annamarie and another one, right? And you're the eldest?"

She nodded solemnly. "I'm thirty-six. Mary Etta's next. She's the brainy one—she's an assistant research chemist. She always loved chemistry—all kinds of science, really. When she was a little girl, I remember…" Her voice trailed off and she yawned again. "Hmm, where was I?"

"You were about to tell me about my new sister-in-law."

"Annamarie. You wouldn't believe what a beautiful baby she was. I used to take care of her because Mama worked at the doctor's office. Strangers would come up and say how pretty she was. Well, actually, we didn't get all that many strangers in Grover's Hollow. The population stays right around nine hundred. People die, people are born, but almost nobody ever moves there voluntarily." She caught him looking at her with those translucent gray eyes and wished she could read his thoughts.

"You were saying?" he prompted.

"Oh. I talk too much. But about Annamarie, I was only trying to explain what she's like. Everybody loves her. Even when she lost six front teeth at one time, she had the sweetest smile." Pausing for breath, she heaved a sigh that caused his gaze to fall from her face to her bosom. Rafe would have to say that proportionally she was just about perfect. A nice, uncomplicated dumpling of a woman who happened to have her own sweet smile, not to mention beautiful eyes and the kind of skin that invited a man's touch.

Not that he was tempted. Not that she'd done anything to tempt him, he had to admit. Just the opposite, if anything, which in itself was something of a novelty. Women had always gone out of their way to catch his attention. He usually enjoyed it. What man wouldn't?

He had a feeling this one would be a lot happier if she'd never laid eyes on him. There was a certain novelty appeal, he had to admit, in being with a woman who wanted nothing more from him than his absence.

She claimed to have been at the wedding—the wedding Rafe had missed. She knew Stu, so he had to wonder just how much had the kid told her about the half brother who had helped raise him. Had he mentioned that Rafe made and lost more money in a single year than some men saw in a lifetime? When a man could afford to lose, he usually didn't. Had that impressed this woman at all? Did anything impress her…anything besides broken bits of purple clamshells?

"Do you like to fly?" he asked. *Go ahead, jerk, spread it on. She's seen the Beechcraft. Now tell her about the other plane back in Tampa.*

"I don't know, I've never flown."

He blinked twice at that. "Everybody flies. It's a lot safer than getting out on the highway."

"You're probably right, but I've never had any real reason to fly anywhere."

That pretty well took care of that topic. "How about boating?"

"Well, I rode in a boat on the New River once."

He waited. "And?"

"And it turned over and my friend had to drag me ashore. He was worried sick about losing the boat— it was a rental—so I sat in the car and waited while he went downriver to catch it."

"And did he?"

"Oh, sure. It had hung up on a snag. I caught a bad cold."

Lady, Rafe was tempted to say, you are no ball of fire when it comes to conversation. "So, what are your hobbies?"

She frowned. Silky auburn eyebrows puckered into worried lines. "Um…I like to read. I've always done a lot of reading. I taught Mary Etta and Annamarie to read before they were old enough to go to school."

It was like pulling teeth. The less she told him, the more determined he was to get behind that placid façade and discover the woman who lived there. It was the challenge of the thing, Rafe told himself. He'd always been a sucker for a challenge. Besides, he was used to women trying to impress him, trying to seduce him—wanting something from him. In the circles he moved in, that was the way the game was played. And when it came to playing the game, he prided himself on being one of the best, making certain first that everyone knew the rules going in.

Molly probably didn't even know there *were* rules.

"What kind of work do you do when you're not cleaning cages and trying not to blush when a parrot calls you a—"

She held up a hand. "Don't say it. I can't believe— I don't even know half the words they say. One's as bad as the other. They egg each other on once they get started."

"Who taught them to talk? Your sister?"

Molly eased a foot out from under her and flexed her ankle as if her leg had gone to sleep. "Heavens, no! Annamarie said they were rescued from a fraternity house after a fire. Nobody would claim them, and Annamarie's fascinated by the way people talk. Birds, too, I guess. She says some of their words are Chaucerian. She wants to do a study of their vocabulary once she finishes with her Ocracoke project. I don't know about Chaucer—it sounds like pure gutter to me."

"Or impure gutter. What kind of work do you do, Molly?"

"I've done lots of things, most of it pretty dull."

He didn't doubt that. On the other hand, no woman

in his experience was an open book. Even his gorgeous, hedonistic Belle had turned out to have a latent nesting urge. Thank God he'd discovered it in time. "Such as?" he prompted.

Molly stiffened her legs out on the sofa and wriggled her toes. She was wearing socks, as Stu's boots had blistered her heels—and until she bought bandages, she didn't care to risk wearing shoes.

"Such as janitor at a grocery store when I was too young to get a regular job. I got paid off in day-old bread and expired meat and produce, which was legal. I think. Anyway, it came in handy and none of us ever got sick. Once I learned simple bookkeeping I did better, but nowadays there are so many different computer programs, and everyone seems to use a different one. I'm a fast learner, about that sort of thing, anyway, but it seems like every time I tackle a new system, it's obsolete by the time I catch on."

She smiled at him, inviting him to share her amusing dilemma. When she forgot herself long enough to let down her hair, so to speak, she was a surprisingly attractive woman. Friendly, warm, engaging. "And?" he prompted, not particularly interested in a recital of her work history so much as fascinated by the way she spoke, using her hands, her eyes and her full, unpainted lips.

"Well. Next came the bank. I've always been good at math, but mostly you just have to be able to read and understand regulations, but anyway, the branch closed when the bank merged and I was redundant. Then I got a job as a stock clerk for a building-supply place. I like the smell of new wood, but the warehouse was full of wallboard and chipboard, all sorts of fabricated materials, and it turned out I was allergic to some of the glues and chemicals. I do—I did—bookkeeping for some small businesses at home.''

Some women touched their hair. It was a classical female gesture. Molly touched her foot. He didn't have a clue what that meant. ''So what happened then? You found an allergy-free zone with an opening?''

She flashed him a quick look that made him feel vaguely guilty. All women liked to talk about themselves. He'd thought he was doing her a favor. It wasn't as if they had a lot to choose from when it came to entertainment.

''I'm sorry. I told you—no, I guess I didn't, but the thing is, sometimes I talk too much. I'm not sure if it's the Irish coffee or nerves, so if you'll excuse me—'' She reached for her book, but he stayed her hand.

''Molly, don't.''

''Don't what? Don't read?''

''Don't make me feel guilty, I'm lousy at guilt.'' He was good at guilt. It was one of the reasons why he was here.

''Oh, for mercy's sake, you're not the one boring *me* to death with a recital of all the dull jobs *you've* ever held in your life.''

''I will if you'll listen. But first tell me the rest of the story of Molly Dewhurst.''

''It'll be Molly Stevens again once I get around to changing it legally, but that's another story.''

''For tomorrow night,'' he said, offering her his most disarming grin. Another thing he was good at—disarming women. Evidently he hadn't lost his touch. He wondered if she'd ever heard of Scheherazade. ''Go on with what you were saying.''

Molly couldn't remember what she'd been saying. She wasn't sure if he was interested or merely pretending. They could both sit around and listen to the parrots, but that was more embarrassing than entertaining. There was a weather radio but the automated voice quickly grew boring. The tiny AM-FM radio got mostly static and country music.

"So—well, my current job is a position, with a title and everything. And I love it, I really do. I'm going to stay there forever, if they'll keep me." Unless Kenny found out where she was and made a nuisance of himself again. His usual tactic was showing up at her workplace to ask for money, perching on her desk, spreading his smarmy charm on everyone within range, making a general nuisance of himself until, embarrassed to death, she gave him whatever she had on her just to get rid of him. A loan, he always called it, promising to pay her back as soon as his luck turned around.

"And that is?"

"And what is?"

"Your present job."

"Oh. Well, my official title is head housekeeper at an assisted-living establishment, but actually I do a little of everything. Aside from seeing that the laundry and cleaning staff do their jobs, and that supplies are kept current, I mean."

Rafe held his empty cup in both hands and stared at the rain-lashed window. The break had been short-lived, with the rain starting up again just after dark. The low was supposed to move offshore tomorrow or the next day, but until then, he was tied down as securely as the Baron. The fishing tournament was officially over, but most of the teams were still trapped here. Besides, he wasn't going to be around long enough to go to the trouble of moving, even if he could find a vacancy.

He tried to think of another question to ask, not that he was particularly interested, but he liked the sound of her voice. It was slower than he was used to hearing, but not quite a drawl. Husky, but not artificially so. He'd had a brief fling with a woman once who affected a husky drawl that had driven him right up the wall. Evidently she'd thought it sounded sexy. It didn't.

"So...what do you do in your spare time?"

"Nothing you'd find particularly interesting, I'm sure," she said dryly.

"I'm easily entertained."

Lifting her cup, she inhaled the lingering aroma of rich coffee and Irish whiskey. "I help with shopping and wrapping gifts for some of the women, and write letters for others and take care of house plants and help fill photo albums for those whose fingers aren't quite as nimble as they used to be. In a way it's almost like having a big family."

A big family. Ironically, Rafe thought, he actually had one, for all the good it did him. Maybe he'd look up another sibling or two once he got back. He'd met one of his father's brood once and felt no connection at all. The kid had been a spoiled brat.

"It's getting about that time again," he said, stretching his arms over his head. Rainy days were perfect for sleeping in, and for afternoon naps...all with the right partner, of course. "I'd better think about cooking us up something to eat. Unless you'd rather go out?"

"Mercy, no, not until the sun shines again. Let's eat leftovers tonight."

"Great. I'll have the asparagus salad and you can clean up the candied yams, spoonbread and Crab Alfredo."

She tossed a pillow at him. "You're a wicked man." She smiled, and in the light of two low-wattage lamps, she looked almost pretty.

Pretty? Hell, she looked almost beautiful!

Almost...

She reached for the stack of junk mail she'd tossed onto the table when they'd come in from the beach. "Let me sift out the catalogs and then you can put this in your room on the desk. Annamarie said chances are there won't be anything that can't wait until they get back."

Rafe watched her hands as she dealt with a stack of circulars, solicitations and catalogs. Nice hands. Small, shapely, with short, unpolished nails and dimpled knuckles. Belle had long, bony hands with long, metallic red nails. She was forever complaining that they didn't make artificial nails like they used to.

A soft gasp drew his attention from her hands to her face. "Molly? What's wrong?"

She looked up, and he tried to interpret the expression in her large, honey-brown eyes. Dismay? Fear?

Five

"Molly?" Rafe's voice, rough with concern, broke through her concentration and she managed to smile.

"It's nothing. Did you mention coffee?"

He hadn't. They'd just had coffee, but obviously the effects of the Bushmill's had worn off. She needed to think, though, and she could hardly do that with him looming over her. "Cream and two sugars, no whiskey," she said with a smile that probably looked as forced as it felt.

Kenny had tracked her down.

Wrong. The post office had tracked her down. Kenny had addressed the letter to her old apartment, where she'd lived after they had separated, and the post office had done the rest. From Grover's Hollow to Morgantown to Elizabeth City, and then on to Ocracoke after Mrs. James at Holly Hills scribbled in Annamarie's box number and zip code. It didn't necessarily mean that Kenny knew where she was now. According to the original postmark, he was still back in West Virginia. And even if he'd had the skill to track her down again, there was no reason why he should want to. Her modest salary covered her own needs only because those were equally modest. The trouble with Kenny was that he couldn't stand having his toys taken away, even when he grew tired of playing with them.

Rafe was still there, stretched out in the easy chair, his long legs crossed at the ankles. He ignored her request for coffee with two sugars and one cream, which was probably just as well. She preferred it that way, but took it black and bitter. Penance for lost cheekbones.

He'd left his shoes on the front porch alongside her borrowed boots, as both pairs were too sandy to bring inside. Molly had found a surprising sense of intimacy in the mutual shedding of shoes and the bare-footed sipping of Irish coffee. Not exactly sexy, but...intimate.

"Want to tell me about it?" he suggested casually.

"What? Tell you about what?"

"What hit you so hard. You went about three shades paler just then."

"Oh, for mercy's sake, I did not." She shuffled the stack of junk mail off onto the floor, still clutching the forwarded legal-size envelope.

"Go ahead and open it. I'll go make more coffee if you want some privacy."

"Go—stay—I don't care what you do. It's nothing, anyway. Nothing important."

Leaning forward, Rafe pulled a copy of the local newspaper, the *Coastland Times,* from the stack on the floor, and pretended to read. Ocracoke's single page was inside. School menus. Board of fisheries report. A poem by a local high school senior. Not a whole lot to engage his attention. He wondered if there was a newsstand on the island that sold the *Wall Street Journal* or even *USA Today*.

He watched as Molly worked the envelope open incrementally. She was frowning, chewing on her lower lip. Whatever it was—threats from a creditor, a ransom note?—it could hardly be all that bad. She wasn't the type of woman to get mixed up in anything too shady.

Or was she? What did he really know about her? She claimed to know Stu, claimed to be Annamarie's sister, but hell, she could just as easily have claimed to be a reincarnation of Mary, Queen of Scots. He had no proof either way. The first time he'd ever seen her she'd been with some guy who hadn't even bothered to see her to the door. Come to think of it, she'd looked upset at the time, even by the single yard light. And that was before she'd even discovered the stranger in her kitchen.

So she knew how to look after the birds. No big deal. Lots of people knew how to take care of birds, although why anyone would want to be around this particular pair escaped him. The cat liked her, but cats could be bought with a treat and a good ear-scratching. Not that he had any personal knowledge when it came to pets. Until a rebellious kid brother had been dumped in his lap, the only dependents he'd allowed himself were a goldfish and a houseplant. When the plant had turned yellow and died, he'd given the fish to the kid next door. Working on a degree and holding down a job as night watchman at a medical supply house, he'd been too busy for further involvement.

That had been just one of several lean periods in his life. Stella had forgotten to transfer the child-care payments when she'd left Stu on his doorstep, so to speak. Meeting his half brother for the first time had left him too rattled to even think about how he was going to manage financially.

The wind-driven rain attacked another side of the house, which meant the wind had shifted. Which meant the nor'easter might finally be moving offshore. Which meant that with any luck, he could be out of here by tomorrow.

Oddly enough, the thought wasn't particularly appealing.

Without even looking at her, he knew Molly had opened her letter. Whoever it was from, whatever it was about, was no concern of his, he reminded himself. But hearing a soft, shuddering sigh, he relented. "If you want to talk about it, I've got broad shoulders and big ears."

She looked up, as if just realizing she wasn't alone, and choked off a laugh. "You have nice ears—not too big, not too small. But no thanks." Her smile cut through a few more layers of the defenses he'd built up over the years without even being aware of it.

"Your call. Look, instead of more coffee, why don't I make us a couple of turkey sandwiches? The sooner we get that carcass out of the way, the sooner we can start over."

Molly said, "Fine." He had an idea she would have agreed to just about anything at that point. Which made him all the more curious.

In the kitchen he laid out the ingredients and

stepped back to survey the possibilities. Turkey, mayo, horseradish, olives, provolone, lettuce—it was only iceberg, but it would do in a pinch. The bread was whole wheat, thin sliced. He would have preferred croissants, but he could compromise. One of the first lessons he'd learned after being left more or less on his own after Stella had dumped his old man and hooked up with her next prospect, was how and when to compromise.

Bread was easy. He set to work slicing and spreading, and pondered adding butter along with the mayo. He decided against it. The lady had a few pounds she'd like to lose, although she looked fine just the way she was. Better than fine, actually.

Which just went to show that he had a few problems of his own. Despite the fact that he had a full social life on tap whenever he was in the mood for companionship, lately he'd been growing restless. Nothing he could put his finger on, just a feeling that life was moving too fast and he just might be missing out on something important.

He was imagining things. The weather had him pinned down. He was stuck in a four-room cottage with a sexy woman and it was screwing up his mind.

Sexy? Molly Dewhurst?

No way. She was simply a nice, wholesome woman with a pretty face, a disarming sense of humor and a ripe, lush body that any normal male would find…interesting.

He stacked thin slices of turkey breast onto bread slathered with mayo, added a touch of horseradish and then artistically arranged the other ingredients. "Work of art," he muttered smugly.

"Did you say something?" Molly called out from the next room.

Glancing around the door into the living room, he saw that she was staring out the window, the letter still in her hands. "I said, work of art. Constructing sandwiches." He topped off the leftover coffee with milk, poured it over ice and carried the tray into the living room. "Later on I'll make us a special dessert instead of dinner, and we can have an early night."

What other kind was there when there was nothing to do? The local pubs weren't worth the effort on a night like this, with the wind blowing a full gale and the roads flooded. If things didn't break by tomorrow, he might have to settle for one of Stu's history books, or something called *Early English Survivals on Hatteras Island.* One of Annamarie's thrillers, no doubt. He'd given it a quick glance, thinking it might be about shipwrecks, but it had to do with exploring remnants of Elizabethan English phraseology along the Outer Banks.

He'd settle for exploring Molly. If he grew tired of that, he would throw together something scrumptious in the kitchen that would tempt her right down to her pretty pink toenails and entertain himself by watching her try to resist.

No, he wouldn't. She didn't need the hassle, not tonight. Maybe tomorrow...

Carefully she refolded the letter and laid the envelope aside. Silently they ate. Rafe couldn't help but notice the way she enjoyed his creation, closing her eyes and sighing. He wished he'd added butter along with the couple of tablespoons of mayonnaise. There was something amazingly sensuous about a woman who truly enjoyed her food.

Later they talked about politics, and somewhat to his surprise, she was well-informed and not at all timid about voicing her opinions. After a spirited discussion of the pros and cons of voter referenda, he made fresh coffee and they switched to sports. Molly loved baseball. He was a football fan. He occasionally played golf. She occasionally watched stock-car races, explaining that the sport had gotten its start with bootleggers trying to outrun revenuers. "One of my great-uncles once operated the biggest still in Grover's Hollow. They say people used to come from all around to buy his whiskey, but he died when revenuers were chasing him up a mountain road and he lost control of his car and went over the side. The strange thing is, it was less than a mile from where my parents ran off the same road and were killed."

How the hell was a guy supposed to react to something like that? Sympathy? Admiration? He opted for changing the subject. "What about fishing? Ever done much of that?"

She shook her head, causing her hair to slither free of its confinement. "It was never a real big thing in Grover's Hollow. Maybe if I'd had brothers instead of sisters, I might have tried it."

"But then, if you'd had brothers instead of sisters, we wouldn't be having this conversation."

She laughed for the first time since she'd sorted through the mail and found the letter that was bothering her. He'd just as soon keep her mind off whatever problem had followed her here, because a relaxed Molly Dewhurst was surprisingly good company. Relaxed, interesting and attractive enough in her own unique way to add the zest of sexual awareness.

A little too much zest. "Tell me about the rest of your family, Molly."

"I've already told you everything there is, even about Great-Uncle Oliver, the bootlegger."

"You left out the part about changing your name to Dewhurst. Stu's wife was a Stevens before she married, wasn't she?"

She picked up a crumb with her thumb and licked it off. "Oh, for mercy's sake, I've done all the talking. It's your turn now. Your life is bound to be more interesting than mine."

"What makes you think so?"

"Your suntan, for one thing. And you fly a plane. And you're a marvelous cook. Most men can't even operate a can opener without cutting their fingers and having to be waited on hand and foot for a week."

Bingo. Another clue. They were beginning to pile up. For a woman who chattered when she was uncomfortable, she didn't impart a whole lot of personal information. And the more she left unsaid, the more she fascinated him.

Maybe *fascinated* was too strong a term. *Mildly interested* was a better one.

Oh, yeah. Nothing like a mildly interested libido.

Sometime in the night he heard a sharp sound, a thump and a soft, muttered curse. He'd been lying awake, wondering what the devil he was doing here when he could be looking over property along the lower mid-Atlantic coast. The southbound Cedar Island ferry was still running. He'd rented the rust bucket for a week.

"You okay?" he called out softly. He was pretty

sure the sound had originated from inside the house, not outside.

"I'm fine. Go back to sleep," she growled.

The rain had stopped, but the wind was howling harder than ever, whistling under the eaves, twisting the branches of ancient live oak trees to scrape against the house. He rolled out of bed and reached for his jeans. Sand gritting under his bare feet, he made his way to the small bathroom that had obviously been added on after the house was built, probably in the late forties. The door hung open. The only way to keep it closed was to hook it. Molly was on her hands and knees peering under the claw-footed bathtub.

Rafe sucked his breath, his hands moving instinctively to echo the sweet curve of her derriere. "Lost a contact?"

"I dropped a bottle of tea tree oil."

"Tell me what it looks like and I'll help you find it."

"It looks like a bottle of tea tree oil," she snapped, reminding him that some women weren't at their best in the middle of the night.

On the other hand, some were.

Molly was obviously of the former persuasion.

"This it?" He raked a small brown bottle from behind the wastebasket and bent over to pick it up. There was a sealed adhesive bandage on the floor, as well. "What are we doing? Performing a little midnight surgery?" She had rolled over onto her behind and was glaring up at him.

Molly on her feet in broad daylight was one thing. Molly on her rump in the middle of the floor at midnight, with one sock on and one sock off, was something else.

"Need some help?"

She said no first, then yes. "My blasted arms are too short! I can't twist far enough around to reach the back of my heel with both hands, and I've already ruined three bandages trying to stick them on one-handed." She looked embarrassed, angry and so damned sweet, he was tempted to offer to kiss her foot and make it well, and then explore any other possible injuries.

But he didn't. There was something about the woman that affected him in a way he had never been affected before. He didn't know quite how to deal with it, but he had a feeling it was nothing to mess around with. Having shared the water with tiger sharks, barracuda and moray eels, he had quickly learned that looks could be deceiving.

She leaned back on her elbows and lifted her bare foot. About a size-five lady's, he figured. Medium. He'd done a stint in a mall shoe store the summer of his freshman year in college.

"You want some of this stuff on it first?" He indicated the small brown bottle.

"Please," she said through clenched jaws. "Just a tad. If you get too much on, the bandage won't stick. That was part of my problem."

"It's going to burn. You've got a big one here, with the top torn half off. Want a little surgery while I'm at it?"

"Just dab on the oil and cover it with a bandage, never mind the flap. It'll either grow back or fall off."

Holding her ankle in one hand, he anointed the blistered heel, smoothed on the bandage and tried not to stare at the length of rounded female leg on the other end. He was breathing through his mouth, somewhat more rapidly than usual by the time he set her foot gently back on the floor. When she started to get up, he offered her a hand.

"Go back to bed," she said in that oddly husky voice of hers. "You've done your good deed for the day. And thank you, Rafe. I could have managed, but this was quicker."

Maybe it was the intoxicating effects of the astringent oil, combined with something sweet and powdery that smelled like sea grape, but he refused to leave her there on the floor. Sheer stubbornness on his part, knowing she wanted him to leave so she could get up with no great loss of dignity. Some women, the long-stemmed ones, could manage to rise in one flowing, balletic movement. Molly was built along sturdier lines, her ballast arranged slightly differently. He found himself wanting to lift her up and hold her until she was steady on her feet, and then carry her back to bed.

His or hers?

Damned if he knew. What he did know was that he'd better think about moving on, weather or no weather. He could always come back for the Baron, or send someone else for it. If he missed Stu he would catch him later, after Sister Molly had gone back to wherever she did her head-housekeeping.

Funny woman, he concluded. Nice woman. He couldn't recall the last time he'd spent this much time in close contact with any woman, even Belle, and felt so comfortable.

Only, comfort wasn't exactly what he was feeling at the moment, which was why he cut it short and told her good-night.

* * *

Rafe had high hopes of getting off the island, but the wind was still howling the next morning when he pulled on his jeans and closed his bedroom window. He had anchored various stacks of paper with giant quahog shells, or else they'd have been scattered all over the room.

Molly was already up. She'd been on the phone. Her expression was puzzling, to say the least. "Problem?" he asked, reaching for the coffeemaker.

She shook her head too quickly. He thought about pressing her, but decided to ease up. Odds were better than even that he'd be able to leave by midafternoon. He'd just as soon not get involved in anything that might mess up his exit.

Once he'd packed his gear, he set about putting the office back in the condition he'd found it. The cot had held stacks of books, notes, audiotapes and a professional looking recorder. Molly had stacked them neatly in the corner when she'd made up the cot. He pondered whether or not to pile them back on the cot and decided against it, in case he needed to stay another day.

The truth was, he could probably have flown out by now, but given the condition of the roads he'd felt compelled to hang around until the water went down enough for Molly to be able to drive. If she decided to go sightseeing and ended up driving off into Silver Lake, he didn't want it on his conscience,

By midmorning the heavy clouds had blown offshore. The teenager next door waded across the yard to drape several small crocheted rugs over the picket fence. Seeing Rafe, she grinned and shrugged. He lifted a hand in greeting. Knee-high boots and navel rings? Cute kid, but he was just as happy not to have another teenager to raise.

The phone rang an hour later, just as they were sitting down to cheese-and-salsa sandwiches. As Molly seemed reluctant to answer it, Rafe grabbed it on the fifth ring. ''Rafe? What the dickens are you doing there? Did I dial your number by mistake?''

''Stu? Hell, no, boy. I came to help you celebrate your birthday.'' Rafe filled him in on how he'd flown in with the makings of a surprise dinner and gotten trapped by one of the notorious low-pressure storms.

''Yeah, the birds are fine,'' he said in answer to the next series of questions. ''Cat, too. Molly? Blistered heel from wearing your boots for a beach walk, but other than that—yeah, I thought maybe later today. Tomorrow for sure.'' There was a long pause, during which Rafe listened to a recital of recently unearthed historical data and the bliss of being married to the world's most wonderful woman.

Molly listened to the one-sided conversation, trying to decipher Rafe's few remarks. Later today *what?* Tomorrow for sure *what?*

He was leaving. The news was surprisingly unwelcome. After only a few days of sharing a cramped cottage with a stranger who delighted in playing diet games with her, she had to admit she had enjoyed herself more than she had in years. He didn't whine, he didn't ask for money and he hadn't once complained that nobody understood him.

The sooner he left, the better, before she got used to having him around.

''Going out?'' Rafe asked. He replaced the phone in its cradle and looked from her to the window and back.

"The water's gone down some. I thought I might, um—go for a beach walk. I mean, as long as I'm here, I want to take advantage of every sunny day. And I want to collect some more shells so that I can take some to everyone at Holly Hills." What she wanted even more was not to be here when he left. That way she couldn't embarrass herself by begging him to stay until Stu and Annamarie returned. "In case you're gone when I get back, goodbye, have a good flight, and maybe we'll see each other again someday."

She was talking too much again. Overexplaining. She would have preferred to leave him with a better last impression, but the most important thing was to get out of range before she did anything stupid. Like begging him not to leave.

"Beach walking sounds good. First decent day since I got in. Why don't I join you?"

Men. She didn't know whether to cry or throw something. "I thought you were so anxious to leave."

"Stu said they'll be heading back early tomorrow. I might as well stay another couple of days as long as I'm here. Once I get back to the Gulf Coast it might be a while before I can get away again."

So they drove the rusted SUV Rafe called the rust bucket, with the bracket of pole holders on the front that gave it the appearance of a snaggletoothed rhinoceros, and parked across the narrow highway from the pony pen. He switched off the ignition and they sat for several moments, watching another flight of pelicans following the dune line. "What's bugging you, Molly?" he asked out of the blue.

"Bugging me? I don't know what—"

"Cut it out. Look, it's none of my business, but you've been distracted ever since that letter came. If you've got a problem that could use a disinterested perspective, I'm offering my services. I know for a fact that when you're in over your head, an outside view can sometimes be helpful.''

She heaved a sigh that steamed up the windows. Or maybe he was doing that. Or maybe it was a joint effort. Rafe could think of a few more pleasurable ways of steaming up the windows, but in this case they were inappropriate. Which was a damned shame, because it might be interesting to see—

''My ex-husband. The letter was from him. At first I thought he'd found out where I am, but that's silly. There's no way he can find out because the post office won't give out that kind of information. Will they?'' she asked plaintively.

He almost lost it then. Almost reached for her in the pure interest of offering comfort.

Yeah, sure, you're a saint, Webber. All compassion. ''Let's get out and let the sun bake out some of the mildew. We'll take it point by point, okay?''

Not until they were leaning into the stiff southwest wind that blew sand across a deserted beach did he speak again. Without thinking, he'd taken her hand, and now he tucked her arm in his and adjusted his stride to her shorter legs. ''So your husband's written you a letter and you don't particularly want him to know where you are, right? Is he stalking you? There are legal measures against that sort of thing.''

''Kenny's not a stalker, he's more of a—well, a leech.''

''Suppose you start at the point where things went wrong. If we take it from there, we should be able to pinpoint the problem and figure out an efficient way to deal with it. I do it all the time.''

As a businessman he operated that way. On a personal level he made a point of remaining uninvolved. If problems arose, he simply cut his losses and moved on, having learned at an early age to avoid messy entanglements. Over the years he'd had to haul Stu off the reefs a few times—the least he could do was offer Molly the same service.

"Well. Here goes. The life and times of Molly Dewhurst. You can stop me any time by holding up a hand." With a funny little half smile, she lit into a recital that skimmed over falling in love for the first time, marrying in haste, all the way to repenting at leisure. Some of it he'd heard before, but because he liked her voice, liked the feel of her at his side, the occasional whiff of baby powder and something wildly exotic, like hand lotion, he listened attentively, putting in a probing question or two from time to time.

"Did you ever think of getting a restraining order?"

"Restraining him from what? Being a pest? Actually, I considered it, but when I tried to think of what I could tell a judge, it didn't sound all that bad. I mean, he wasn't exactly stalking me. It was more of an embarrassment than a threat. He'd come by where I work and hang around, talking to everyone else in the office, making a general nuisance of himself. I always got lectured once he left. Once the coffee money disappeared, and I'm pretty sure it was Kenny, but that was hardly a felony. Somebody stole a fur-collared men's coat from the cloakroom last November, but if it was Kenny, I never saw him wearing it. There were some other things, little things that hardly seemed important at the time, but mostly it was that he was always hanging around, making a nuisance of himself and whining to anyone who would listen about stupid laws and stupid rules and stupid bureaucrats. First thing I knew, I'd be out of another job.''

''Honey, there are laws against that, too.''

''I know,'' she said with a sigh. ''There's a government agency for just about everything, but I hate having to ask some bureaucrat to solve my personal problems. And anyway, I didn't see it as a pattern when it was happening. I'd just get another job and start over again. Things would be all right for a while, and I'd tell myself I'd imagined it, but then he'd show up again, needing money or begging to move in with me.''

''Didn't he have a job?''

''He was always on the verge of something big.''

Rafe knew the type. They usually worked harder at avoiding work than most nine-to-fivers ever did at work.

They walked for a couple of miles, passing three groups of fishermen and several vehicles, including a familiar-looking green pickup truck. Molly was reminded all over again that when it came to romance, she'd do better to take up needlepoint. The only men who showed an interest were interested for all the wrong reasons. She didn't know what the right reasons were, but she knew what they *weren't*. And she was tired of being a one-woman support system for losers.

By the time she accepted a hand up into the rust bucket she was already starting to regret having confided in him. Rafe could tell by the way she twisted her hands in her lap and avoided his eyes. Bless her heart, did she think she was the first woman ever to pour out her worries? Sooner or later, most women he knew intimately did. Mostly it was petty stuff, occasionally family troubles. Now and then an earth-shaking decision such as whether or not to have plastic surgery, and whether implants would have the same sensitivity as real breasts.

Rafe didn't always know the answer—sometimes there wasn't a definitive answer—but if listening helped, then he was available. He liked women. If a woman he'd once had an affair with came back after several years and asked for his help or his advice, he was glad to do what he could. Usually they didn't, but once in a while someone did.

But this, he reminded himself, was Molly. If Stu stayed married to Annamarie, then they'd be family. It might be smart to go easy here, on account of Molly's idea of family and his own weren't even in the same ballpark.

"Well…thanks for listening," she said as he pulled up in front of the house between her car and a red convertible.

Six

They could hear the parrots all the way out in the yard. Pete's *"Bad-ass, bad-ass!"* fought for airtime against Repete's string of four-letter words. Molly said, "Oh, Lord, the neighbors," and hurried up onto the porch.

And then she stepped back and looked over her shoulder. "Rafe? The front door's open. Did you say Stu and Annamarie were coming today or tomorrow?"

He was beside her by that time. "Tomorrow," he said quietly. "Know anyone who drives a red convertible?"

She shook her head slowly. "But you know how parking is around here. Wherever there's a space, you squeeze in. Anyway, Sally Ann says there's practically no crime on the island, at least in the wintertime."

"In case you hadn't noticed, it's no longer winter. Go next door and stay there until I come for you."

"I'll do no such thing, I'm responsible for those birds. And Shag. Annamarie would die if something happened to that cat. She's had him forever."

Clasping her shoulders, Rafe eased her to one side. His breath was warm on her cool face, but there was no hint of warmth in his eyes. "Humor me, will you? It's probably nothing, but—"

"Molly? Is that you, darling?" The voice came from inside the house.

Even before he saw her reaction, Rafe had a pretty good idea who their intruder was. He had personally locked the front door, but if he knew Stu, his brother had probably left a key stashed outside in the most obvious place. As a kid he used to lock himself out at least once a week.

Still gripping Molly's shoulders, he whispered, "Recognize the voice?"

Wordlessly she nodded.

"The ex?"

Her eyes said it all.

"Shall I invite him to leave?"

She sighed. "Could you just wait outside for a few minutes? I don't want to have to explain you."

His shrug said, "It's your call," but he didn't release her, not until she looked pointedly at his hand on her shoulder. And by then it was too late.

A guy wearing an unseasonable fur-collared top-coat and a politician's smile appeared in the doorway. The smile disappeared. "Moll, who's this?"

Rafe, who had always considered himself fair and unbiased, despised him on sight.

"Just a—a friend of a friend." Under her breath

she hissed, "Don't you dare call me darling! Don't call me anything. Just go away!"

"You wouldn't answer my letter, you wouldn't return my calls—what am I supposed to do when my wife ignores me?"

Rafe shrugged and headed out to the SUV where he raised the hood and pretended to tinker with the battery cables while the other two stood on the porch talking. If they went inside, he'd have to think of something else, but no way was he going to leave her alone with some jerk who followed her down here and claimed they were still married.

Unless they were. Rafe had only her word that she was divorced. She could have lied about the semi-stalking ex-husband. Lied about the letter. She could be faking the whole scenario. Maybe she was just into games, trying to reignite a burned-out marriage. He'd known people who never told the truth when a lie would serve as well.

But Molly? No way.

The guy didn't look dangerous, but Rafe had learned a long time ago that looks could be deceiving. Any man who would sponge off a woman was obviously short on integrity, not to mention pride.

So he pulled out the dipstick and checked the oil while he was under the hood. For whatever reasons, she didn't want the fellow here or she'd have taken him inside. They were still on the front porch. He could hear them talking, but with the parrots running through their X-rated repertoire, he couldn't quite make out the words. The guy was sweating. He'd like to think it was because Molly was royally reaming him out, but it was probably the coat. To say he was overdressed was an understatement.

Molly wore twin patches of pink on her cheeks. In her damp, sandy denim with her hands on her hips, she looked more than a match for any man, but he had a feeling she was the kind of woman who led with her heart instead of her head.

Frowning down at the distributor cap, Rafe spread his hands on the rusted fender and reminded himself that it was none of his business. Just because she'd confided in him, that didn't mean he had to take on her battles. Hell, any cop would tell you that domestic affairs were trickier than an octopus at a pickpocket's convention.

Still, he couldn't just walk away. In the few days they'd been together he'd come to know her pretty well. They had talked about everything from politics to poetry. They both liked limericks, only he didn't know any clean ones and she wouldn't admit to knowing any of the other kind. Along the way he had come to know the woman lurking underneath that plain exterior.

Actually, the exterior wasn't all that plain, merely understated.

Rafe had no way of knowing if women reacted the same way men did when faced with an unexpected situation. The adrenaline rush. How the devil had she managed to hook up with such a loser in the first place? The guy whined, for Pete's sake! He dressed for effect, not comfort, which said a lot about him right up front. Probably caught her at a weak moment and played on her sympathy. With a woman like Molly, it would be a surefire technique.

"Aw, come on, honey, don't be like that." Now that the birds had run down, both the words and the tone were clearly audible. "For better or worse, re-member? You promised."

"Kenny, I said no, and I mean it. I have barely enough gas and grocery money to last out the month. I certainly don't have enough to lend you. And if you get me fired from one more job, I'm going to—to—"

Rafe had heard enough. Wiping his hands on his handkerchief, he sauntered back up to the porch. "Molly? Is there a problem?"

Trapped. That was the only way to describe the look on her face as he moved to stand beside her. He slipped his arm around her waist, presenting a solid front, and there it was, right on schedule. Rafe had never run from a fight in his life. Had a few battle scars to show for it, but damned if he was going to stand by and let this creep talk a good woman into anything against her will. "Hi, I don't think I caught your name. Rafe Webber here." Crocodile smile, extended hand. Dewhurst stared at the hand with distrust, but Rafe wasn't about to let him off the hook.

Reluctantly the smaller man accepted the gesture. At the feel of that soft, limp handclasp, Rafe, not usually given to impulse, did something totally out of the blue. "I'm Molly's new husband. Why don't you go on inside, babe, and heat up the coffee. I'll join you in a minute."

Her jaw fell. She stared at him as if he'd suddenly sprouted a horn in the middle of his forehead, then abruptly she turned and fled.

Had Rafe lost his mind? Molly asked herself, standing stock-still in the middle of the tiny kitchen. Or had she? How on earth was she supposed to deal with *two* men, both claiming to be her husband?

Kenny wanted money, of course. Kenny always

Play **LUCKY HEARTS** for this..

exciting FREE gift !
This surprise mystery gift
could be yours free

when you play **LUCKY HEARTS!**
...then continue your lucky streak
with a sweetheart of a deal!

1. Play Lucky Hearts as instructed on the opposite page.

2. Send back this card and you'll receive 2 brand-new Silhouette Desire® novels. These books have a cover price of $3.99 each in the U.S. and $4.50 each in Canada, but the are yours to keep absolutely free.

3. There's no catch! You're under no obligation to buy anything. We charge nothing—ZERO—for your first shipment. And you don't have to make any minimum number of purchases—not even one!

4. The fact is thousands of readers enjoy receiving their books by mail from the Silhouet Reader Service™. They enjoy the convenience of home delivery...they like getting the best new novels at discount prices, BEFORE they're available in stores...and they love their *Heart to Heart* subscriber newsletter featuring author news, horoscopes, recipes, book reviews and much more!

5. We hope that after receiving your free books you'll want to remain a subscriber. But th choice is yours—to continue or cancel, any time at all! So why not take us up on our invitation, with no risk of any kind. You'll be glad you did!

Visit us online at
www.eHarlequin.com

- **Exciting Silhouette® romance novels—FREE!**
- **Plus an exciting mystery gift—FREE!**
- **No cost! No obligation to buy!**

YES!

I have scratched off the silver card. Please send me the 2 FREE books and gift for which I qualify.
I understand I am under no obligation to purchase any books, as explained on the back and on the opposite page.

With a coin, scratch off the silver card and check below to see what we have for you.

SILHOUETTE'S

LUCKY HEARTS GAME

326 SDL C6QR

225 SDL C6QM
(S-D-OS-06/01)

| | | | | | | | | | | | | | | | | | | | |

NAME   (PLEASE PRINT CLEARLY)

| | | | | | | | | | | | | | | | | | | | |

ADDRESS

| | | | | | | | | | | | | | | | | | | | |

APT.#   CITY

| | | | | | | | | | | | | | | | | | | | |

STATE/PROV.   ZIP/POSTAL CODE

Twenty-one gets you 2 free books, and a free mystery gift!

Twenty gets you 2 free books!

Nineteen gets you 1 free book!

Try Again!

The Silhouette Reader Service™—Here's how it works:

Accepting your 2 free books and gift places you under no obligation to buy anything. You may keep the books and gift and return the shipping statement marked "cancel." If you do not cancel, about a month later we'll send you 6 additional novels and bill you just $3.34 each in the U.S., or $3.74 each in Canada, plus 25¢ shipping & handling per book and applicable tax if any.* That's the complete price and — compared to cover prices of $3.99 each in the U.S. and $4.50 each in Canada — quite a bargain! You may cancel at any time, but if you choose to continue, every month we'll send you 6 more books, which you may either purchase at the discount price or return to us and cancel your subscription.

*Terms and prices subject to change without notice. Sales tax applicable in N.Y. Canadian residents will be charged applicable provincial taxes and GST.

BUSINESS REPLY MAIL

FIRST-CLASS MAIL   PERMIT NO. 717   BUFFALO, NY

POSTAGE WILL BE PAID BY ADDRESSEE

SILHOUETTE READER SERVICE
3010 WALDEN AVE
PO BOX 1867
BUFFALO NY 14240-9952

NO POSTAGE
NECESSARY
IF MAILED
IN THE
UNITED STATES

wanted money. He used to nag her to get a retail job so he could use her discount. She'd been far more interested in health benefits, only, as things turned out, once she was married she was never able to keep a job long enough for benefits to kick in. To think she had once worked for the same company for seven years. But that was before she'd met Kenny.

She reached for the coffeemaker, changed her mind, and scowling, marched back to the front door in time to hear Rafe say, "If you hurry, you can just about make the next ferry. I wouldn't bother to call first, just show up at the office, tell him Webber sent you and—yeah, wear what you're wearing now. It's perfect."

Halfway down the steps, Kenny glanced over his shoulder. His face was flushed. Molly couldn't tell if it was fear or excitement she saw there, but whatever Rafe had said seemed to have worked. He was leaving.

"I know where you got that coat," she called after him. "You ought to be ashamed of yourself!"

"Ashamed?" Rafe murmured, both dark eyebrows lifting. To the man hurrying down the front walk, he called out, "Do we understand each other, Dewhurst?"

"Yeah, sure thing. No problem. Wish you luck— you don't have to worry about me, I'm outta here."

Rafe draped an arm over Molly's shoulder and smiled benignly. There was nothing at all benign about the way his gaze followed the departing man.

"Did I step over the line?" he asked once the red convertible was out of sight.

"Probably."

"I tend to be impulsive."

"That, I doubt."

His smile broadened into a grin. "Hey, it takes practice. I'm working on it."

"Whatever you threatened him with, it seems to have worked," she said, but for a second she'd glimpsed another side of Rafe Webber. Where men were concerned, she had learned the hard way that what you saw was not necessarily what you got.

"Hey, I made a suggestion, that's all."

She very much doubted if that was all, but she let it go. "I'd have promised anything just to get rid of him. Can you believe he wanted me to cash in my measly little IRA? He says he's in the stock market now, and he has inside information on a sure thing."

"Last I heard, insider trading was against the law."

"I don't think that will slow him down. And I seriously doubt if he's any kind of an insider. Kenny just likes to collect snippets of rumors and weave them into his own little fantasy." She sighed. "Poor Kenny. He knows better than to try threats on me. They won't work, because I know him too well."

"What works?"

"Bribery." Molly sighed again, and then she chuckled. Rafe had forgotten to remove his arm from her shoulder, and she tried to ignore the heat and weight of it. "He knows just how to embarrass me until I give in and let him have whatever money I have on me just to get rid of him. Trouble is, I can't afford to buy him off any longer. I'm trying to build a retirement fund, but it's not easy."

A retirement fund. It had been his experience that women, including his own mother, counted on men to secure their future. But then he'd never met a woman like this one. Not knowing quite what to say, he changed the subject.

"What'd you mean about the coat?"

"Only that I'm pretty sure he stole it."

"Do tell." And then, for no reason at all, they were suddenly grinning like a pair of conspirators.

Molly said, "I don't know how you managed to get rid of him—threats or promises—but I doubt if he believes we're married."

"What's not to believe?"

Lifting her eyebrows, she stared at him. "Me? You?"

Before she could react, he leaned over and kissed her on the tip of the nose. "Don't worry. I didn't threaten to take out a contract on him, I only suggested that a change of climate might work wonders for that flushed skin of his. Mentioned the name of a modeling agency down in Tampa that was always on the lookout for men with his looks and a flair for wearing good clothes."

Molly almost strangled. "You *what?* Kenny can't afford to go to Florida. He probably couldn't even get off the island if it weren't for the free ferry." The funny thing was, though, that she could almost see him as a male model. His favorite sport had always been trying on clothes.

"Depends on the motivation, I suppose. What do you say we eat out tonight?" Rafe suggested, thus changing the subject from the man he had subtly threatened by dangling the carrot, then showing the stick.

"I thought you were leaving this afternoon."

"As long as I'm here I might as well hang around another day. The honeymooners will be back tomorrow, and there's no telling when I'll be able to free up time for another visit.''

Another few hours, then. There were dozens of questions she wanted to ask. It occurred to her that Rafe knew all there was to know about her, from the fact that she was a sucker for a sob story, to every job she'd ever held, to the fact that she could never remember the punch line of a joke long enough to repeat it, and that she had a real weakness for anything containing coconut. He probably knew what size she wore, because she hadn't gotten around to clipping the tags from inside her new clothes.

What did she know about him? Nothing. What he did when he wasn't cooking up temptation or flying around in that fancy plane of his, whether or not he was involved with a woman. Or with several women. She wanted to ask just how he'd talked Kenny into that hasty, red-faced departure, because she had an idea there was a bit more to it than he'd let on.

A modeling agency? What did he know about modeling agencies?

On second thought, it might be better if she didn't know.

Molly spent the rest of the afternoon giving the birdcages a thorough cleaning. Or as thorough as she dared without risking a finger. Rafe went out. She didn't ask where, nor did he tell her. At least he didn't say goodbye, which meant he'd probably be back in time for their dinner date.

Mercy. She had a date with the man. Her fancy denim outfit with the nailheads and embroidery was damp and sandy. The laundry basket was full of clothes waiting to be washed and line dried once the weather cleared up, as the cottage didn't run to a dryer. Which left her with two choices. Her oldest jeans and a ratty sweatshirt, or the only dressy outfit she had brought with her, a flattering gored skirt, ankle length, with a long turtleneck pullover, both in black.

An hour later she fastened small gray pearl studs to her earlobes. She rouged hollows under her cheekbones, or where her cheekbones would be if they ever surfaced again.

Tomorrow Stu and Annamarie would be here and she'd be free to leave. Tomorrow she would go back to her apartment and wait until the renovators were finished at Holly Hills, and then she could throw herself into all sorts of projects. Starting a library or seeing if she could get someone from the college interested in holding a few classes in creative writing, or genealogy. Oh, she had all sorts of creative ideas that didn't exactly fit her job description. Maybe she would see if Holly Hills needed an activity director. They had a physical therapist and once a week, a crafts instructor, but maybe she could—

And maybe she'd do well to keep her feet on the ground and her head out of the clouds, Molly reminded herself.

They met in the living room. Rafe was breathtaking in khakis, a white shirt and a dark blazer. Which was something else she was going to have to deal with sooner or later. Sooner would be better. Sooner might not leave any lasting scars.

They took her car. Rafe drove. The water had gone down considerably, but it was still slow going. They passed Delroy's Pub and Molly thought of her last dinner date. From this moment on, she had a feeling she'd be measuring every man she met against Rafe Webber. It was a depressing thought for a woman who was determined not to be depressed.

"This suit you?" Having chosen one of several restaurants on the island, Rafe tucked her hand over his arm as they waited to be seated. Her smile nearly rocked him back on his heels. He wouldn't have thought black would be her color, not with her muted coloring, but it brought out the red highlights in her hair, the golden tint of her skin and the amber glow of her eyes. She had a lot to offer some lucky man, he told himself. Some deserving nine-to-fiver who would give her a home and children and all the things a woman like Molly needed.

She ordered the cheapest thing on the menu. He ordered a sampler tray for an appetizer. When the platter of shrimp, scallops and seviche came, she looked at it suspiciously. He forked out a grilled shrimp, dipped it in the tangy sauce and held it to her lips. "Open up, Molly."

She snapped the shrimp off the fork and chewed as if she were angry.

"What's wrong. You wanted the fried cheese? We can have that with coffee for dessert."

Reluctant laughter lit her eyes like an unexpected streak of sunlight. He stared, bemused. "I'm sorry. I guess I'm still worried about Kenny. I wish I knew how he located me. It's awful to dislike someone you once cared enough about to marry. Doesn't say a whole lot about my judgment, does it?"

"How well did you know him before you married him?"

"Not well enough, obviously. I saw what I thought was a handsome man with excellent taste who was involved in a lot of important business deals. I couldn't believe it when he asked me to marry him three weeks after we met.''

''Love at first sight.''

''Infatuation. Followed by confusion, followed by disillusionment. Followed by a few other things I'd just as soon forget. At least I learned my lesson.'' *Did you now, Moll? What about Jeffy? What about this man? What do you really know about him after all?*

Rafe fed her another shrimp, and then a scallop dipped in tartar sauce. She closed her eyes, savoring the sweet, tangy blend of flavors. ''No more men, hmm?''

''No more marriage,'' she corrected, and sampled the seviche. ''I end up feeling sorry for the men I'm attracted to, and it just doesn't—oh, this is so good!— it just doesn't work out.''

''You feel sorry for Dewhurst?''

''Can't help it.'' She took a delicate bite from a golden brown hush puppy. ''It can't be easy, knowing you're such a loser, always having to pretend because you're afraid other people will see through you.''

''How did you get to be so wise at your age?''

She laughed outright at that. ''Wise? Uh-uh, not me. Mercy, how can you say that when you've just met one of my major mistakes? Here, try this stuff. I don't know what it is, but it's delicious.''

''Raw fish.''

Her eyes widened. ''No it's not. Raw fish is sushi, and it's all rolled up in little balls with capers and things sticking out the ends.''

''This was marinated in lime juice. The acid— you'll pardon the expression, coagulates the proto-plasm. No calories involved.'' He didn't mention the oil. He was beginning to enjoy feeding her, tempting her, enjoying her sensuous pleasure. "Conch seviche's a lot better, but this isn't half-bad."

Fascinated, Rafe watched her golden brown eyes widen and then close as she savored another forkful of the cold fish salad. It occurred to him that he had never known a more sensuous woman. Or a more intriguing one. Her appeal, he was beginning to discover, had nothing to do with fancy clothes or being seen in all the right places with all the right people. Unlike most of the women he'd known intimately, she didn't wait to find out what he thought about a subject and then fall all over herself agreeing. Molly argued. She could talk intelligently about a surprising number of topics, expressed curiosity about as many others and wasn't afraid to admit she knew nothing at all about still others.

By the time the waiter brought their dinners, they had demolished the appetizers. Without asking, Rafe lifted two hush puppies, a crab cake and several fried scallops off his plate and onto hers. "You need all the seafood you can get while you're here. It's got all sorts of health benefits."

"It also has a zillion calories when it comes breaded and fried."

"Have I told you how beautiful you look tonight?"

"No, and don't bother." She sampled a fried scallop and closed her eyes in ecstasy. "I'm overdressed, for one thing. Look around. Practically every other woman in here is wearing jeans and big, dangly earrings. Way cool, as Carly would say."

"That's Carly of the belly-button jewelry, right? The neighbour's daughter? Oh, yeah—I'd trust her fashion expertise any day."

Molly helped herself to a bite of his fried sea trout. "She's only fifteen years old. Give her time."

"Stu was fifteen when I got him to raise. We didn't even speak the same language."

"You did a good job. I don't know him all that well yet, but I like him a lot. I trust Annamarie's judgment." Better than her own, she could have said, but didn't.

"You know about his trust fund?"

"Not much. Only that some day he'll probably get some money."

Rafe nearly swallowed a bone. "Yeah. That's about the size of it."

"He's going to be a great history teacher. You can tell he loves his subject, just listening to him talk about it."

Rafe didn't particularly care to speculate on what would happen when his half brother turned thirty-one. Unless he was a hell of a lot stronger than he looked, it was going to make a big difference. His wife would have a lot to do with how things ultimately turned out. "What do you think, fried cheese and coffee or key lime pie?"

"What? Oh—none for me, thanks. You go ahead, though."

"You didn't touch your dinner." Made some pretty big inroads on his, but her broiled chicken and green salad had been barely touched. "What's wrong, Molly? Are you still worrying about Dewhurst?"

"Kenny? No, I think you opened up a whole new world for him. Of course, it probably won't work out, but…"

"But?"

"Rafe, you did all anyone could ask and more. And

I thank you, I really do. If he shows up again, then I'll deal with it, okay? I've certainly had enough practice.''

''Just out of curiosity, how do you usually handle it?''

She toyed with the idea of not answering, but he had more or less made it his business earlier. ''When I have it, I give him money. I refuse to let him move in with me, not even when he claims he'll have to sleep on the street because he can't afford security and first month's rent on another place. The sad thing is that Kenny's really fairly smart, in a way. He'll get a job, work until the first payday, then quit and look for something better. He's— I guess you could say he's a perennial dreamer.''

''I guess you could say he's a perennial hustler,'' Rafe said dryly.

''He borrows money to buy lottery tickets. Every time he opens the door he expects to see someone from Publisher's Clearing House.'' She sighed and propped her chin on her linked fingers. ''According to someone who used to know his family, he was a beautiful little boy. His mama spoiled him rotten, gave him everything he ever asked for, convinced him he was special and made excuses for him, no matter what he did. It was never his fault, you know? And then, once she was gone, poor Kenny found out that as far as the rest of the world was concerned, he wasn't so special after all.''

Rafe watched the candlelight reflected in her eyes. Large, warm, honey-colored eyes.

''You have to feel sorry for someone like that.'' That soft husky voice undercut the noise of cutlery, china and laughter all around them.

"You do?"

"You can't despise a child," she said patiently. "Kenny just never grew up."

Rafe shook his head slowly in amazement. How the hell did you respond to a statement like that? Instead, he changed the subject by waving a waiter over and ordering a whole key lime pie to go.

By the time they got back to the cottage, Molly regretted having not done justice to her chicken. She had eaten the raw fish thingee and Rafe had made her sample his seafood platter. She couldn't be hungry. But sharing the cottage with a whole key lime pie was dangerous. When her emotions were involved, she couldn't count on her common sense to protect her. In some ways she was no wiser than Kenny.

Rafe headed for the kitchen to put away the pie. Molly draped her shawl over a chair and tucked a few loose tendrils of hair back into her French twist, then decided to change into something more comfortable. Not that she wasn't perfectly comfortable in her black knit outfit, but key lime pie wasn't her greatest weakness. Rafe had told her she looked beautiful. They both knew it wasn't so, but just to be on the safe side, she'd better change into her grungiest everyday clothes. She was who she was and Rafe was who he was, and no matter what he'd told Kenny about being her new husband, that was one twain that would never meet.

If Kenny came after her again and wanted to know where her husband was, she would tell him—

Nothing. She didn't have to tell him one darned thing. In case Rafe was worried, she wanted him to know that she had no intention of perpetuating the

lie. Feet on the ground and cards on the table, that
was her policy from now on.

Back in her jeans and a sweatshirt that had seen
better days, she marched into the living room intent
on clearing the air. Rafe beat her to the draw. "Uh-
oh, you've got that look in your eye."

"What look?"

"Militant. Is something bugging you? You're not
still upset because I told whatsisname we were married, are you? Molly, where've you been for the past
fifty years?"

"Not in your circles, obviously. And anyway, he
couldn't have believed it."

"Something's on your mind. I haven't seen that
Molly-on-the-warpath look in days."

"I told you, there's nothing on my mind. I'm
happy as a clam, so happy I'm going to have a bite
of that pie. Do you want me to cut you a slice?"

He studied her with curious eyes. "I'll wait a
while."

She made it a tiny slice. Just a teensy sample. Crisis
food, she told herself now that the crisis had passed.
Back in the living room a few minutes later, she chose
one of the two straight chairs, set her pie on the book-
shelf and launched her attack. "All right, we can
agree on one thing—you're leaving tomorrow, but
chances are, we might run into each other from time
to time. You being Stu's brother and me being Annamarie's sister and all. So—"

"You think the world's going to come to an end
if people think we've slept together? And you're how
old, Molly—thirty-five?"

"Thirty-six," she snapped.

Touched and amused, Rafe watched her struggle

with the idea. Color bloomed on her cheeks, competing with the twin streaks of rouge. Racing stripes, they were called among the women he knew. "Honey," he said softly, "this is the twenty-first century. Women have the vote, they hold public office—they pretty much do as they please, and no one holds them accountable." Except maybe for their kids, he thought, but the bitterness he'd once felt toward his own mother had long since lost its edge.

"So? What's your point?"

"My point is this. Unless you've got a few more jealous men lurking in your background, I think we can forget having to explain anything. I don't know about your sister, but Stu won't have a problem with our being here together."

"Oh. Well, I wasn't actually concerned. I mean, for goodness' sake, we're both certainly old enough, and—well, people live together all the time and nobody gives it a second thought. It's just that things are different in real small towns, and anyway—"

"Molly."

"And even in Grover's Hollow we have cable, so it's not like we—"

"Molly," he said again, but she was on a roll. Thank God he'd tossed sheets over the cages or the birds would be adding their two cents' worth. Covered, they were somewhat quieter.

Rafe levered himself out of the sagging easy chair. Planting himself in front of her, he said her name again and then he captured her hands and drew her up into his arms. "Is this what's got you so uptight? I believe it's called sexual tension," he whispered just before his mouth came down on hers.

Rafe had it pegged. It *was* called sexual tension, and it had been simmering just under the surface all day.

Seven

She tasted as sweet as she looked. She felt just the way a woman should feel—soft and solid and warm. Resilient. Not fragile and bony, all angles and edges. The novelty of it alone was enough to encourage him, even before her arms crept around his neck and she started making squeaky little noises in her throat.

Incendiary. That was the only word to describe what was happening. At thirty-eight, Rafe thought he had long since passed the age where testosterone overruled common sense. There were plenty of reasons for not getting involved. Trouble was, they weren't getting through to his brain.

Compulsion was another word that applied. This compulsion to go on holding her, tasting her, feeling her warm body pressed against his, inhaling the essence of Molly Dewhurst. A unique blend of sexiness and innocence.

It caught him off guard, the lack of artifice. Granted, she was a desirable woman, and granted, they'd been sharing close quarters. Granted, too, the sexual awareness that had been lurking just under the surface, feeding on itself. Chemistry happened.

The trouble was, there just might be something more than chemistry involved. Not only did he find himself wanting to explore every delectable inch of her body, he wanted to reach inside her mind and explore the warm, disarming, engaging woman that was Molly Dewhurst. That was downright scary.

"Mercy," she whispered breathlessly. She was clinging to his ears with both hands as her eyes slowly opened to stare wonderingly at his face. "Did you just kiss me, or did I imagine it?"

His amused response held an edge of desperation. "If you don't know, then maybe my technique is getting rusty."

"Oh, no—it's just fine! I mean, you do it really well." She closed her eyes and bopped her head against his chest. "Why not just shut up before you make a complete fool of yourself, Molly Lou?" she muttered fiercely.

The cat was sleeping on the sofa. With one hand, Rafe waved him away. The sofa was too narrow for what he had in mind, but then that might be a good thing. With any other woman in these same circumstances, bed would have been the next logical step. But this was Molly, not any other woman. He wasn't exactly sure of the rules here; he only knew that the old rules didn't apply.

One thing was clear—that loser she'd been married to had obviously been too damned self-centered to know how to treat a woman. Rafe knew how to treat a woman. He'd made it something of an art. Trouble was, Molly deserved more than quick, convenient, a-good-time-was-had-by-all sex. And that was all he could offer.

"Uh—maybe I'll have some pie after all," he said, gently disengaging himself. The cat leapt back up on the sofa and glared at him as if to say, *Hey, if you're not going to use this thing, buddy, butt out!*

"Oh. Pie." She shook her head. "I don't know why I feel like crying."

Gut punch. "You feel like *what?*"

"Don't mind me, you go ahead and have your dessert. Mine's around here somewhere. Would you put it in the refrigerator for me? I'm not hungry after all. I should be—I hardly touched my chicken, but... It must be the weather. That and Kenny and—and everything." Her voice spiked dangerously. She was babbling again.

Rafe recognized the signs by now. She was embarrassed. Her voice was too cheerful, her eyes were too bright—her lips were still swollen from his kiss. He didn't know whether to eat pie or make love. He knew which he'd rather do, and it didn't necessarily include meringue. He stood there, watching her as if he were a member of a bomb squad faced with some strange new explosive device.

"Molly?" She waved him away, but it was too late. One fat tear broke the barrier of her thick lashes and slipped down her cheek. "Ah, honey—don't do that," he growled.

It was all she needed. For all of ten seconds she stood there, arms at her sides, sniffling and gasping convulsively. Then Rafe opened his arms and she turned blindly into his embrace.

Molly was beyond embarrassment, but there was no way she could hold back. What she needed more than anything else in the world at this moment was comfort. Pure, physical, nonjudgmental comfort. She had long since outgrown the kiss-it-and-make-it-well stage, but some needs were elemental.

She didn't even want to think about why she so desperately needed comforting. Kenny was only the smallest part of it. It had far more to do with a basic need that had been growing inside her for too long. "Do you mind—would you mind just holding me?" she asked, struggling for some vestige of dignity. There was nothing at all sexual about the request. That had been only a momentary...aberration.

Still holding her, he shooed the cat away again and settled down on the sofa. Still cradled in his arms, she turned so that she was resting against his chest, her arms draped around his shoulders. That way she could hide her ruined face in his throat until she managed to regain control of her emotions.

"I'm so embarrassed," she mumbled into his collar. She was ruining his shirt, getting it all damp.

Something rumbled in his throat. No words, just a comforting sound. She shoved her fists up under his arms, where it was warm and safe and cozy. Then just as she was beginning to get herself in hand again, the dam burst, releasing the flood that had been building for too many years since her parents had been killed driving in a blinding rain on a mountain road.

There'd been no time to grieve then. She'd had to be strong for her sisters, to deal with the funeral home, the lawyer, the preacher and all the people who had tried to smother them with kindness. Then there'd been the woman from social services, and the insurance people. Her father's policy had lapsed when payments had fallen behind. A wonderful man, kind and funny and loving, he had never been good with details. An avalanche of details. She remembered crying, but grieving was far more than crying, and there'd been no time for anything more than tears shed in the middle of the night, wrenching sobs stifled in her pillow so her sisters wouldn't hear.

She'd had to find a second job, which meant working seven days a week to pay off the lawyer and her father's debts. And then there were braces and tuition and all the extras that kept piling up faster than her meager earnings could cover.

Finally, just as her responsibilities had begun to ease, Kenny had come along, and in a moment of inexcusable weakness she had married him.

It hadn't taken long before she'd realized that her charming prince was largely a figment of her imagination, but the deed was done. For better or worse, she'd been determined to stick by her vows. In Grover's Hollow, things like marriage vows were taken seriously. Things might have been different if she hadn't gotten pregnant. They hadn't planned it. Kenny didn't particularly like children. Probably because, as she realized later, he was still too much of a child himself and didn't want competition.

He'd been having trouble holding a job because, as he put it, either he was overqualified, or the boss was unreasonable or there was no room for advancement. Whatever the excuse, none of his jobs lasted more than a few weeks. The more Molly came to know the man she had married, the more she'd worried. Morning sickness struck hard and early, and that hadn't helped. Then in the space of three weeks her employer had gone bankrupt and Kenny had quit his job driving for a vending machine company because it was beneath his dignity. A week later she lost her baby. Riddled with guilt, she'd been unable to cry, afraid that once she started she might never be able to stop.

And now, of all times, she'd had to start. "I'm so sorry," she blubbered.

"It's all right. Just go on and get him out of your system."

He thought she was crying over Kenny. "I wish he'd drive off the end of the ferry and drown," she muttered against his soggy collar.

"I'm not sure you could handle the guilt if it happened," he said, sounding almost amused.

"Have you evermore got me pegged?" She even managed a wet chuckle. "Knowing Kenny, he'd land on a shoal and have to be rescued, and then sue the rescuers and the ferry company for mental anguish and ruining his new coat."

"Sounds like a real prince."

"Don't laugh. If he thought we were really married, he'd probably sue you for stealing his meal ticket."

"I can see it now, The Molly Stakes. Cross lawyers and come out fighting?"

She snickered. And then she burst out laughing. It felt incredibly good, even though her eyes were burning and her nose was stopped up, and nothing had really changed. "It's not funny, you know. Now that he knows where I work, he's probably going to hang around Holly Hills and make a nuisance of himself, and first thing you know, I'll be more trouble than

I'm worth and they'll find some reason to let me go. It's happened too many times in the past.''

''He'd do that even thinking you've remarried?''

She uttered a ladylike snort. ''He'd never in a million years believe someone like you would marry someone like me, even though I've been gainfully employed for nearly twenty years and once won a prize for my practically fat-free chicken pot pie.''

Rafe's arms tightened around her. An intoxicating blend of his cedarwood shaving soap and her baby powder, enhanced by the heat generated by two adult bodies, eddied around them. Somewhat to his amazement, Rafe realized that he could easily see himself married to Molly. She was…comfortable. Surprisingly good company. Sexy in a way that was both earthy and innocent.

Get a grip, man. This is your half brother's sister-in-law!

He tried. He thought about Stu, who might be neck-deep in trouble again, depending on what kind of woman this Annamarie turned out to be. That could turn out to be a messy situation if Rafe allowed himself to get involved with Molly.

He thought about certain personnel problems waiting for him back at the Coral Tree Inn. He thought about Belle, his ex-mistress, who was probably busy making babies at this very moment. Which brought him full circle to the problem in his arms.

The way Rafe saw it, Molly's biggest problem, aside from that jerk she'd been married to, was a badly bruised self-esteem. For which the jerk could probably take full credit. And while Rafe was in a position to do something about it, there were certain hazards involved, one of which was the fact that he might not be able to maintain his objectivity.

Her fingers uncurled and slipped around to his back. Couldn't she tell what was happening to him? His heart was thundering like a cattle stampede, he was breathing like a locomotive headed up a steep grade. Not to mention certain other obvious clues.

He really should pull back before things got too far out of control. "Molly?"

"This feels so good. Isn't it the most wonderful feeling in the world, being held by someone bigger and stronger than you are?"

"I wouldn't know," he said with a wry grin.

She laughed, a husky, whispery sound that registered in the pit of his belly. *Patience, man. You're in control here. See that you keep it that way.*

Her knees were drawn up beside her. Beside him. Rafe had a feeling that somewhere a fuse was burning dangerously short. "For just this little bit of time," she whispered, "I don't have to think about tomorrow. I don't have to worry about whether or not Kenny's going to be waiting for me once I go back to Holly Hills. For now, I can just stay right here and...glow."

"Glow?"

"Mmm. That nice, drifty feeling you get just before you fall asleep. Sometimes when I have a big problem, I put it under my pillow just before I fall asleep and when I wake up in the morning, the answer is there waiting for me. It's like leaving a door open in your mind."

"Uh-huh. Yes, well—I've got a little problem, but I don't think I'll find an answer under my pillow."

"Sex, you mean."

Mentally he slammed on the antilock brakes. "I do? I mean, it's no big problem...honestly. Nothing I can't handle." A long, cold shower and a fast flight out at daybreak should just about do it. The honeymooners could wait.

"I'm sorry. I didn't mean to embarrass you, but—well, I couldn't help notice, and if there's anything I can do—"

He swore. Broke it off quickly, not wanting the birds to get any ideas, but— "Dammit, Molly, do you always blurt out the first thing that pops into your mind?"

"Not always—actually, almost never, but it's a good policy. Feet on the floor, cards on the table. It saves misunderstandings."

"Yeah, well, I have to tell you, it just might land you in trouble one of these days. Another man might take you up on your offer."

"I didn't offer—well, I guess I did, didn't I? But you know what I mean."

"No, I don't. Suppose you tell me."

"Well, I meant...that is, I might be partly to blame—I mean, I know how men are about these—um, physiological things?" She tipped her face back far enough to peer up at him. Far enough for him to see the fiery color flare in her cheeks again.

"You mean a man might get aroused just from holding a beautiful woman in his arms and kissing her—feeling her breasts pressed against his chest, breathing in the scent of her skin, imagining what it would be like to—"

She covered his mouth with her hand. "I didn't mean—"

"Feet on the floor, cards on the table, Molly."

"Oh, my mercy, all right! Me, too, for what it's worth. I mean, I was, too—feeling that way. Only, with a woman, men can't tell."

"I can tell." His voice sounded as if someone had a hammerlock on his larynx.

"You can? How?"

"First clue? Your pupils are dilated. Second? Your pulse is too fast. Third? You're breathing as if you've just run a three-minute mile."

"All right, you made your point." And then, "I am?" she asked wonderingly.

"You're still here, right? You could have walked away. And then there's this," he murmured as he lowered his face to hers.

One kiss merged into another. By the time they came up for air, Molly's sweatshirt was on the floor. Rafe's hand-tailored shirt was unbuttoned and tugged free of his belt. Shag had had his way with Molly's pie and was licking the empty saucer across the floor.

No one noticed. No one cared. Somehow they managed to reach the bedroom without barging into anything. Rafe left the door open so that light from the living room fell through the doorway. Molly flung back the quilt just before they collapsed onto the bed, then Rafe tugged it over them both. He was burning up. She was shivering, but probably not from cold.

Fleetingly she considered confessing that she wasn't particularly experienced. She had slept with only one man in her life, and hadn't especially enjoyed it. Cards on the table and all that.

But the thought was lost when she felt his fingers on the buttons of her jeans. Frantically they finished undressing each other. Hands tangled, the quilt ended up in a heap on the floor, but by that time neither of them had need of the additional warmth.

Rafe felt on the floor for his khakis and managed to extract his wallet from the hip pocket. There should be a single condom there, left over from his pre-Belle days. One should do it. It wasn't as if this would lead to anything more, it was just a case of—

Of letting off steam, he told himself. Bleeding the pressure down to a safe level.

And then Molly touched him and his brain shut down. Her hands were small, her touch tentative, but he stiffened and caught his breath.

She snatched her hand away. "I'm sorry, I didn't mean to—it was an accident."

He captured her hand and brought it to his lips. "Molly, Molly, don't apologize. This is for both of us. I just don't want it to end too fast."

"No, of course not, I understand. I won't do anything or say anything to—"

He had to laugh. Here he was, so damned hard he ached with it, and all he could do was lie there laughing. It did nothing at all to relieve the tension. Turning onto his side, he drew her close and eased his knee between her thighs. Her flesh was surprisingly cool. He was hot as an afterburner. She lay perfectly still for several moments, her uneven breathing the only sign that she was as aroused as he was. Rafe slid one hand up between them and tipped her chin up so that he could study her face.

"Molly? We don't have to go through with this if you've changed your mind. A nice, cold midnight swim and I'll be just fine." He vaguely recalled thinking those same thoughts not too long ago. Back to square one. How the hell had that happened?

"I want to."

Her voice was so soft he was afraid he'd misunderstood her. And then he caught on. And swore. "He wanted you silent and passive. Is that it?"

She swallowed hard and nodded, her hair brushing his chin. "Oh, baby—oh, sweetheart, that was his loss. I could almost feel sorry for the poor bastard, but I have an idea he might have put you through some rough times, even more than you let on." He lifted her thigh and eased it over his hip so that they were nestled together in breathtaking intimacy. "Talk. Touch. Tell me what you want, Molly—we're equal partners in this. Your pleasure only doubles mine."

And when she didn't react immediately, he lowered his lips to her breast. "Tell me what you want. Do you like this?" He suckled her gently, and then not so gently. Her nipples were amazingly responsive. "What about this? How does it make you feel?"

He could tell without words how it made her feel. Her toes curled against his shins, her hips moved as if she couldn't get close enough, and when he slipped one hand down between them and found her, she reacted instantly.

And then, somehow, they shifted until it was her lips on his nipples, her fingers toying tentatively with the base of his throbbing erection. As if she were afraid of exploring further.

"Rafe?"

Between clenched jaws, he managed to answer her. "Yeah—oh, yes!"

"Do you feel anything when I kiss your breasts?"

"Let me put it this way, sweetheart—" He could barely control his voice, but in the interests of freeing

her of inhibitions, he went on. "Had a house once—
lightning struck a tree just outside, ran in on some
buried wires. Burned the insulation off the inside wir-
ing, blackened an entire wall and blew off a few
switch plates. Feeling your mouth on my nipple
is...comparable."

"It's all connected, isn't it?"

"Yes'm, that it is. Breast bone connected to the,
uh—other bone. And I have to tell you, if you go on
doing what you're doing, you're going to blow a few
major circuits."

He moved over her then, and even in the near dark
he could see her smile. White teeth, shining eyes.
Lowering his face, he murmured against her mouth
as he parted her and eased into position. "Molly,
sweet Molly, what am I going to do with you?"

Her hips lifted to meet him, welcoming him into
her body, and to his amazement she uttered a breath-
less chuckle. "I hope...that's a rhetorical...question.
Oh, yess-s. Please..."

One slow, measured thrust. And then another. And
then there was no holding back, for either of them.
Molly began to whimper as the fiercest of all pleas-
ures gathered strength and fed on itself like a wildfire
inferno, until it ended in one mindless explosion of
profound pleasure.

Still holding her sweat-slick body in his trembling
arms as the earth slowly settled back on its axis, Rafe
became uneasily aware that something had changed.
Over the past twenty-odd years he had had sex more
times than he could recall, and enjoyed almost every
occasion. He always took care to see that his partners

shared his enjoyment and he invariably parted on good terms with his lovers.

Except in the technical sense, Molly was not a lover. And that was part of the problem—he didn't know exactly what she was. She didn't fit into any of his neat pigeonholes. Her ego had been bruised. She'd been needy, and he'd been here at the right time. One thing had led to another and they'd ended up in bed.

Where was the harm in that? he rationalized. She had enjoyed it as much as he had, if those kittenlike whimpers and that single, wide-eyed yelp had been any indication. If he'd snapped his fingers and produced a light show on the order of the aurora borealis, she couldn't have looked more dumbstruck. You'd think she'd never climaxed before.

Too exhausted at the moment to locate his clothes and beat a strategic retreat, Rafe lay there beside her in the double bed and stared at the ceiling. This was going to take some careful diplomacy. In the space of a few days they had met, gone from suspicion to armed truce, to guarded friendship...and now this.

Whatever *this* was. He still didn't understand it. Molly wasn't his type. He wasn't in love with her. Liked her, sure, but hell, he liked all the women he slept with.

Could it have been the laughter? Come to think of it, he couldn't remember laughing with a woman right up to the moment when he'd buried himself inside her. He'd have thought laughter would have dampened the fire.

If laughter was all it took, then he'd just made a discovery that would put him right up there with Edison, Fessenden and the Wright brothers.

He needed to get out of here. Needed to go for a

long walk on the beach. Needed to get as far away from the warm, sweet-smelling woman beside him as possible so that he could examine this thing clearly and logically from all angles. Nothing had really changed. They'd slept together, period. As consenting adults, both unattached and in their right minds, where was the harm in that?

She stirred beside him, and her hair tickled his chin. "I was just thinking, Molly. Maybe I'd better not wait around much longer. I can always come back to see Stu later on. We'll probably run into each other from time to time—holidays, maybe. I used to try and make Thanksgiving and Christmas special for the kid—for Stu, that is. Maybe we can—"

"Don't spoil it by feeling guilty, Rafe. It was about the nicest thing that's ever happened to me."

He could almost sense her smiling in the darkness. Her voice took on a special note when she was pleased about something. "Yeah, well…"

"I thought they were making it up, you know? The people who went on and on about how it felt to—well, I don't care for the clinical terms, but you know what I mean. Reading about it is one thing, but actually—you know—experiencing it, that's something else."

He wanted to gather her in his arms and hug her all over again, but didn't dare risk it. His body was already beginning to react to the feel of her warmth beside him, not to mention the heady scent of sex and baby powder. Besides, he'd used his single condom.

"You don't have to stay here. In my bed, I mean. If you'd rather not—I mean—"

"Molly?"

"What?"

"Hush up and go to sleep."

She sighed. It was a smiley kind of sigh. He could tell by her even breathing when she drifted off to sleep. He was on the verge of drifting off himself when the phone rang in the other room.

Eight

Rafe held the phone in one hand, his pants in the other, and listened silently for several minutes. By the time Molly joined him, wearing only his discarded shirt, which was the first thing she'd grabbed, he had managed to get his pants pulled on and was struggling one-handedly with the zipper.

"What's wrong?" she whispered. "Who is it?" Her mind taut with concern, she was struck all over again by the sight of his lean, bronzed body. No matter how often or how rarely she saw him over the years to come, she would never be able to forget the fact that except for a narrow section around his hips, he was tanned all over. That his body hair was several shades darker than the thick crop on his head. Everything about the man was incredibly arousing. From practically her first glimpse, when she hadn't known him, hadn't believed him, hadn't trusted him, she'd been aware at some bone-deep level of that powerful physical attraction.

"Never mind that—I'm here, okay? Yeah, we've met," he said dryly. With one arm he drew her closer to his side and held her there while he spoke tersely into the receiver. "We'll be there in— No, I can't fly out until first light. The landing strip's not—"

"What's wrong?" she whispered.

"You're sure? Level with me. Are you all right?"

"Rafe, what's wrong?" she whispered fiercely. "Who is it?"

He owned a hotel. He probably had dozens of people working for him. Something must have happened back in Florida.

"You said we. Was that you and me, or did I misunderstand?" Of course she'd misunderstood.

He replaced the phone in its cradle and stood for a moment, visibly gathering his thoughts. By this time Molly was truly uneasy. Whatever had happened— wherever it had happened—Rafe was leaving. Going back to Florida at first light. Leaving her here with two birds and a cat and the rest of her life to get through without him.

The thought was devastating.

"How long will it take you to pack?" he demanded.

She stared at him in confusion. "Pack what?"

"Enough for a couple of days. This next-door neighbor—do you think it's too early to wake her up and see if she can take care of the menagerie for a day or so?"

"Sally Ann? She works for the ferry department— she has to get up early. Rafe, what's going on?" Not

Florida, then. Which must mean— "Has something happened to Annamarie?"

Rafe related the bare essentials, which was all he knew. "They were involved in an accident, they're both basically all right, but they're being kept for observation. Save your questions for later, when we're underway. We've got about an hour to wrap things up here. Then I'm headed for the airport, with or without you."

He made another quick call to someone named Mike. Molly didn't wait around to hear what was said. Calling on years of practice, she shoved her emotions into a dark corner of her mind to be dealt with later. First, a quick shower, then she dragged her suitcase out from under the bed and tossed in a few essentials. Every few minutes she would call out another question. "Are you sure neither one of them is seriously hurt?"

"I'm not sure of anything except that they're both able to talk more or less rationally," Rafe called back from the next room. "She said the car didn't catch on fire until after they'd both crawled free."

Catch on fire! In the act of pulling on her one decent pair of jeans. Molly staggered and fell against the bed. "Why didn't you let me talk to my sister?"

"Because she was upset and she kept arguing with Stu on the sidelines, and I figured a four-way conversation would only delay us. Lock the windows and turn off the heat, will you?"

"Down, not off. The birds, remember?" She zipped up her jeans and struggled into her black turtleneck. By the time she had snapped her bag shut and dealt with her hair, the sky was showing a hint of color. Light shone from the kitchen window of the cottage next door. Molly hurried over to explain to Sally Ann about the accident. "Stu and Annamarie are both all right as far as we know, but they've been admitted to Chesapeake General Hospital for observation."

"Get going, honey, don't you worry about a thing. Carly and I will take care of everything."

"I'm pretty sure I can be back in a day or so. Even if Rafe wants to stay on, I'll have him fly me back here and—"

"And nothing. You just go, girl. We'll play zookeeper for as long as it takes. You just show me where everything is before you leave."

The two women hurried back to the cottage, where Molly wrote down the routine, stacked Shag's canned food on the counter beside two containers of seed mix and opened the refrigerator to point out the bird's chopped vegetables. She showed Sally Ann how the cages worked and told her about washing and refilling the water cups. "Annamarie says they don't bite, but I've seen what they can do to a chicken wing poked through the bars. Watch your fingers."

"I'd take the cat home with me, but with the new puppies, maybe I'd better not."

"He's fine outdoors as long as it's not raining too hard. I really owe you for this, Sally Ann."

"You bet you do. You're going to have to take one puppy for every day you're gone once they're weaned." She grinned to show she was only half-serious.

A sleepy-eyed Carly wandered over just as Rafe tossed the two bags into the rust bucket. Wearing only an oversize T-shirt and a pair of fur-lined boots, she looked years younger than the spike-haired, body-pierced teenager he had met once before.

"We'd better get underway before the weather changes again," Rafe said, his gray eyes dark with concern.

Carly yawned, stretched and scratched her neck. "You're flying?"

He nodded. She said, "Coo-wul." And then, "Can I feed the birds while you're gone?"

"It's up to your mother, but I warn you, their vocabulary is X-rated."

"Coo-wul!"

Finally they got away. One look at Rafe's closed face and Molly decided her questions could wait. She tried to focus on Annamarie's situation, but her mind kept straying back to the man beside her.

To think that little more than an hour ago she had been lying in his arms, naked and sated, dreaming warm, fuzzy dreams. Now it was if she didn't even exist. Molly told herself he probably had dozens of women. What wealthy, successful, handsome, charming man didn't? She could hardly expect him to be swept off his feet by a middle-aged, overweight housekeeper from Grover's Hollow, West Virginia.

And yes, she thought dolefully, if seventy-two could be considered elderly, then she was truly middle-aged. The fact that Rafe was even older was immaterial. The rules were different for men.

Her sidelong gaze lingered on his profile. Even frowning, his blunt, angular features redefined male beauty. Hard to believe he and Stu were related. Sweet, shy Stu with his turned-up nose and freckles, who blushed and sometimes stammered under social pressure. By the time he had made it to the altar to stand beside his gorgeous bride in her homemade wedding gown, his boutonniere had been dangling and his bow tie askew. The first time she'd met him, her maternal instincts had stirred to life, though she was only about ten years older than he was.

The instincts Rafe stirred were altogether different, she thought as he slowed down to negotiate a puddle that stretched across the narrow highway. She had a feeling she had just committed a catastrophic blunder. She would like to think that if she had it all to do over again, she never would have slept with him, but an innate sense of honesty refused to let her get away with it. If he were standing before her in a lineup with one hundred of the world's handsomest men, she would have picked him out immediately. There was simply something about the man that got to her. However, this was not the time to analyze it, much less try and deal with it. It would simply have to wait.

The plane was ready to go when they arrived. Rafe checked several things, both inside and out, while a gangly youth lugged their two bags over and shoved them inside. Rafe slipped two folded bills into the hand of the boy, who grinned and said, "Anytime, Cap'n."

Molly didn't even try to breathe as they taxied down the narrow runway, only a stone's throw from the ocean. Eyes closed tightly, she felt the plane lift off and quickly bank around to head north. Opening one eye first and then the other, she clutched her stomach and uttered a soft moan.

"Seat belt too tight? Keep it fastened anyway, okay?"

"It's not the seat belt. It's the breakfast we didn't take time for."

"Open your eyes and look at the horizon. Take a few deep breaths."

Dutifully Molly opened her eyes and peered through the Plexiglas. She drew in a deep breath, and then another.

"Don't hyperventilate," Rafe said over the drone of the engine. "Just look and enjoy."

Remarkably enough, she did just that. Fascinated by the brand-new perspective, Molly forgot all about her queasiness. But before she could appreciate the scenery, she needed answers to the questions there hadn't been time to ask earlier. "Were they on their way back here? What was it, a blow-out? Is Stu a good driver? Because Annamarie's never been all that good. It took three tries before she could even get her license." She covered her mouth. "Don't tell her I told you that. She was so ashamed. I don't know why I did, only—"

He covered her hand with one of his, and she gasped and cried, "Keep your hands on the steering wheel, watch where you're going!"

"Relax, Molly. I won't let anything happen to you. And your secret's safe with me."

"What secret?"

Grinning, he said, "That Annamarie had some trouble getting her license and that you can talk the tail off a kangaroo when you're nervous or uncomfortable."

She was quiet for all of thirty seconds. Then, in a tone of wounded dignity, she said, "Well."

"Here's all I know. There were three vehicles involved. The driver of the dump truck has some broken bones and possible internal injuries, Stu has a mild concussion and three broken bones in his left hand.

Unfortunately he's left-handed. Your sister is basically okay, as far as—''

The plane veered to avoid collision with a flight of geese, and Molly caught her breath and gripped the edges of her seat. Rafe slanted her a quick grin. ''Look down.''

''With my eyes open? Are you crazy?''

But she opened her eyes and looked, and when he pointed out the darker stain on the water and told her it was a school of fish, probably channel bass, she shot him a skeptical look. ''Trust me,'' he said, and she looked again, seeing nothing at all that resembled a fish.

''There. That's not so bad, is it?''

''What, you mean flying with my eyes open? The fact that I'm up here miles above a shark-filled ocean with no visible means of support? Or the fact that your brother has a concussion and a bunch of broken bones and my sister is probably falling apart, even if she's not physically injured?''

Or the fact that we made love, and for the first time I discovered what it's all about, and it probably won't ever happen again?

''How about all of the above?''

''How about concentrating on getting us there?''

The plane was noisy, but surprisingly steady. After a while, Molly relaxed enough to take in the glorious spectacle of sunrise over the chain of narrow barrier islands, an intricate pattern of dark lacework against a background of fiery gold and coral.

Rafe absorbed the scenery as he did every nuance of sound or vibration. He had been flying for more than twenty years. Sometimes he flew as a means of getting from point A to point B. At other times he flew to free his mind of clutter and allow himself to concentrate on the big picture.

Now all he could concentrate on was the woman beside him. Stu's marriage would probably fail; marriages in their families inevitably did, which meant he might never see Molly again. But regardless of what happened in the future, he knew he would never forget her. And that bothered him, because he'd never before had a woman get to him as quickly as she had. Not even Belle, whom he genuinely liked. Certainly not the woman he'd been married to briefly, before he'd wised up and figured the odds.

Molly was...Molly. Feet on the ground, cards on the table.

Her feet might be on the ground, he told himself with tender amusement, but her head was definitely in the clouds. For a thirty-six-year-old divorcée, she was incredibly naive. A sleeping beauty who was just beginning to wake up. The fact that he might have played a part in her awakening gave him an inordinate sense of proprietorship; at the same time it scared the hell out of him.

Noticing how absorbed she was in the panorama below, he banked to allow her better visibility. This time she never even grabbed the seat to hold on. After a while she said softly, ''This is a season of firsts for me.'' Rafe leaned closer to hear, catching a whiff of shampoo and baby powder. She raised her voice and said, ''I don't know if I told you, but it's my first trip to the beach. And this is my first flight, and last night was the first time I ever—'' She slapped a hand over her mouth.

''The first time you ever what?''

''Nothing.''

"You want me to start guessing? The first time you ever *what*, Molly?"

But Molly wasn't about to admit that it was the first time she'd ever slept with any man other than her husband. As for that other thing that had happened, all she could say was that a blaze of sunrise reflected in the water and viewed from the cockpit of a small plane paled in comparison. "The first time I ever met a bird that could curse in three languages."

He laughed. She knew that he knew she was lying, but he was gentleman enough to let her get away with it.

The trip seemed endless. It dawned on Molly that she was moving faster than she had ever moved in her life—another first—yet the earth seemed to creep by below.

"So strange," she murmured. He couldn't possibly have heard her, much less have known what she was talking about. All the same, he reached over and covered her left knee with his right hand, and this time she took comfort in his touch and didn't even yell at him to mind what he was doing.

When they finally landed, Rafe sent her off to find two coffees and a couple of bagels while he took care of the plane. "Meet you at the car rental desk. I'll bring the luggage," he told her, and instructed her on how to get her there.

Airports were another adventure, but by the time she found the ground transportation area, Molly had had her fill of excitement. It had begun to sink in that Annamarie might be more seriously injured than she'd admitted. What about internal injuries? Why else would she be kept for observation?

It didn't help to tell herself that both her sisters

were grown up now. They no longer came running to her to fix every hurt from a stubbed toe to a broken heart. Annamarie had a husband now; she didn't really need her big sister. And Mary Etta was on the verge of getting herself engaged, but then, Mary Etta had always been more independent than Annamarie. In some ways, she was even more independent than Molly was. With Molly, independence had been mostly pretense born of necessity, something she had only recently admitted to herself.

Nevertheless, being accustomed to worrying, Molly continued to worry. By the time she met Rafe at the car rental desk, she was sick with it. "I want you to tell me everything," she said, handing over a cup of weak, lukewarm coffee and a bagel. "I'm strong enough to handle the truth, whatever it is, so don't try to protect me. Besides, I'll find out everything in a little while, and if you've lied, I'll never trust you again. Why did Annamarie insist on talking to you and not me? It's because she knew I'd know, isn't it? I can always tell when she's trying to hide something from me. Her voice sounds different, like she's reading from a script or something."

He dealt with the rental agent, then led her outside, transferred their bags and handed her into the late-model gray sedan. "She talked to me because I answered the phone. As for whether or not she was hiding anything, you know her, I don't. I've never even met her. Whatever we find when we get to the hospital, we can deal with it, all right? Just keep saying to yourself, 'They're the kids, we're the grown-ups.'"

Dutifully Molly repeated, "They're the kids, we're the grown-ups." She drew in a deep, shuddering breath. "Rafe, did you ever get the feeling after your mother left Stu with you that you were just acting the part of an adult? You were scared stiff, but you had to pretend like crazy to keep him from finding out you didn't know all the answers?''

"You, too, huh? Most of the answers I didn't know by then, I found out in a hurry. A few I'm still working on.'' He chuckled softly as he stopped for a red light. "I had a teacher once in the seventh grade who barely managed to stay one lesson ahead of the class. I know how she felt.''

"I can't remember how many times I pretended to be calm and steady and reasonable when I was so scared, I was sick to my stomach.''

He nodded. They followed the signs to the hospital and found a parking space not too far away from the main entrance. When Rafe leaned across her to unfasten her seat belt and Molly caught a hint of his cedarwood shaving soap, it struck her all over again—that stunning affinity she felt for him that she had never felt for another man, not even the one she had married. Dear God, what had she done, besides shattering her concentration just when she needed it most?

A few hours ago she had been naked in bed with this man, doing and feeling things she had never in her wildest dreams imagined doing or feeling. And now, here they were, acting as if it had never happened. As if she didn't know about the scar on his left thigh where a stingray had stuck him and the barb had had to be cut out.

As if he didn't know about all her stretch marks, all the convexities on her body where she would have dearly loved to have concavities. Her rounded belly, for one. Her full cheeks, without a single sign of a cheekbone, for another. She was the plump one, and he was about to meet the gorgeous one. Even as a little girl, strangers would stop to admire Annamarie. Molly had always taken pride in both her sisters, because they were special and she loved them both dearly. They were both enough younger so that sometimes they felt more like her children than her sisters.

Just once, though, she would like to see a man look at her with the same awestruck expression Annamarie never failed to inspire. Just once.

And just this one man.

Please God...

They asked directions and assured Reception they were family. "I'm his, she's hers," he explained. It was enough to get them onto the elevator at least.

Annamarie was pacing outside in the hallway. She rushed forward as soon as the elevator doors opened. "What took you so long? Oh, Molly, I've been so worried—no, no, I'm sorry—I know it must have been awful trying to get through rush-hour traffic, and...you must be Stu's brother. I'm his wife. That is, I'm Annamarie. I'm Molly's sister."

"I would have recognized you anywhere."

"You would?" Both Molly and Annamarie spoke at the same time.

Rafe's smile came on slow and gathered strength. "Yeah, you're a lot alike."

Before Molly could pursue the matter, Annamarie grabbed both her hands and pulled her aside. "I'm sorry, Moll. We should have waited at least until morning." She turned to Rafe and explained. "It's this habit we all have, you know. Not just family, but half the people in Grover's Hollow. Whenever anything goes wrong, everyone calls on Molly to sort it out. When we were growing up, even before Mama and Daddy died, Mary Etta and I used to depend on her. Mama was never what you'd call a hands-on parent. I think Mary Etta and I were afterthoughts—or maybe accidents. Molly was always there, though. She stood up for us and looked out for us—she even made my wedding gown. Did she tell you?'' Rafe opened his mouth to speak, but the exquisite creature with the eggplant-colored bruise on her forehead rushed on. ''Anyway, when all this awful mess happened, naturally the first thing I thought was to call Molly. I just didn't know what else to do. I mean, here we are in a strange city with no car, no clothes— all our notes and the film Stu shot—'' Her face suddenly crumbled and Molly opened her arms.

Over the shoulder of his sobbing sister-in-law, Rafe met Molly's eyes and nodded. ''See what I mean?'' he mouthed silently. ''You're just alike.''

He left her to figure it out while he went in search of his brother's room. He'd recognized Annamarie easily from her wedding pictures. Although she was somewhat the worse for wear at the moment, she looked more like a Hollywood starlet than a linguist. More like a luxury beachfront condo than a two-bedroom cottage with little more than the basic amenities. More like a pedigreed pooch with a rhinestone collar than a pair of ragged, profane parrots and a lazy tomcat.

Rafe decided to reserve judgment on the newest member of the family. When it came to the Stevens women, what you saw was not necessarily all there was. He seemed to remember hearing about another sister who was some kind of research scientist. Hadn't paid much attention at the time because it hadn't seemed important to learn all there was to know about what would probably turn out to be only a temporary alliance.

In the space of a few days it had become vitally important. Molly was what—seven and nine years older than the two youngest sisters? Which meant she'd have been a young teenager when they were just starting school. Their parents had still been alive then. Funny thing though, he had a feeling that however they'd turned out, Molly was largely responsible.

She had made the wedding gown? All that white satin and lace? When the hell had she had time?

Dammit, it was about time people stopped using her and began appreciating her for what she was— one of the sweetest, kindest, most patient, most responsible, most generous women he'd ever had the good fortune to meet.

Not to mention one of the sexiest.

Stu, wearing a thin white turban, was sitting in a chair by the window, staring morosely down at the cast on his left hand. He glanced up when Rafe stepped inside the room. "Boy, did I screw up this time."

"I'm afraid to ask what you mean."

"Old chimneys. You know me and old chimneys. One look at a burned-out hearth and I get to wondering who lived there, and when, and what the living conditions were like when the house was first built. We'd just passed a set of rock ones and I started to say something to Annie, and whamo!"

Whamo. Rafe could remember any number of whamos in his kid brother's past. There were countless skateboard whamos, fortunately with full protective gear, the TR-6 whamo that had doubled his insurance rates, not to mention any number of spectacular surfing wipe-outs. Once Stu had stopped trying to live up to his older brother's example and accepted the fact that he was never going to be an athlete, he'd settled down nicely to become a fairly serious scholar.

Rafe did his best to reassure him that the accident hadn't been his fault, and that even if it had—Rafe hadn't read the report yet, so he didn't honestly know—that these things happened. The kid had enough to deal with without taking on the burden of guilt. "That's what insurance is for. You, uh, you have kept up your premiums, haven't you?"

Glumly the younger man nodded. "Annie sees to all that kind of thing. She's good at paperwork."

"Great. You can trade off, then, because you're good at—"

"Screwing up."

"Knock it off, will you? You must be good at something, to get a beauty like Annamarie to marry you."

Stu's smile started slowly and broadened into a full-blown grin. "Yeah, well...I don't like to brag, but..."

And then the women were there, and there were more formal introductions to be made and plans to be laid. By the time Rafe and Molly left, promising to return during evening visiting hours, Rafe had a pretty good idea of what had to be done. Molly had a list of her own. Outside the hospital, it occurred to Rafe that they hadn't yet secured a place to stay. There were a lot more options here than on Ocracoke Island, but still...

"First priority is finding a bed. I don't know about you, but I didn't get a whole lot of sleep last night."

Molly blushed. Seeing it, Rafe wanted to wrap her in his arms and hold her until the rest of the world went away. Instead, he did his best to ease her embarrassment. "What do you say we hunt up a good restaurant first? I have a feeling we're both going to need to keep up our strength."

She rolled her eyes, and he had to laugh. After a few moments, Molly joined him, and he said, "That's what I like about you—your sense of humor." And then he shook his head. "It's not *all* I like about you—don't misunderstand me. What I meant was—"

"Rafe?"

"Yeah."

"Did anyone ever tell you you talk too much when you're ill at ease?"

"It must be catching."

"That's right, blame someone else. Now hush up and let's go find that restaurant, all right? I'm in the mood for fried chicken and lots of mashed potatoes, with maybe coconut pie for dessert."

There were times, Molly told herself, when calories simply didn't count.

Nine

Molly yawned all the way to the hotel. She was uncomfortably full, because another thing she did besides talk too much when she was upset or worried or ill at ease was eat. She tried to keep pretzels on hand—the fat-free kind—because they crunched so good, but she'd been known to devour a whole bag in one sitting. Pure nerves, but that didn't help the end result.

"A suite?" She gaped at the luxurious surroundings the minute they were alone. "Rafe, that's five whole rooms! It must cost a fortune!"

"Bathrooms don't count."

She shot him the kind of look such a remark deserved, and he shrugged and tossed his jacket at the velvet love seat. "Call it market research if it'll ease your conscience. I'm involved with a couple of hotels—I need to keep up with what the competition is offering.''

''You could have done your market research at Ocracoke instead of moving into a cottage that's not much bigger than this—this—'' She indicated the comfortable lounge that separated the two bedrooms, each with a private bath.

''No vacancies, remember?''

''I wonder how hard you really looked.''

''What, you think I wanted to be stuck there with you?''

She shook her head. They were at it again. Where Rafe was concerned, there was no such thing as a moderate, reasoned response. Almost from the first, every cell in her body had been aware of the man. If she were fifteen years old with typical teenager roller-coaster hormones, it might have been understandable. But she was a thirty-six-year-old divorcée, considered by practically everyone in Grover's Hollow to be seriously, dependably mature. Of the three Stevens sisters, she was said to be the only one with a lick of common sense.

Great. So now the sensible sister had gone and fallen in love with a man who never would have given her a second look if they hadn't been stuck together in a five-room cottage. She would simply have to fall out of love. It might not be easy—it was probably going to hurt like the very devil, but eventually she'd get over it.

At least she could take pride in one thing—her taste in men had improved enormously, she thought as she explored the closets and the bathroom amenities. She was too embarrassed to admit that although she had stayed in motels before—the economy kind where you had to go outside and locate the machines if you got hungry or thirsty—she had never stayed in a real hotel.

Shampoo and conditioner, bubble bath and body lotion, a hair dryer, a sewing kit—and mercy, there was even a phone in the bathroom and a bathrobe hanging on the back of the door. If she'd needed a reminder of the vast gulf between a man who owned an airplane and a hotel, and a woman who had never even been inside either until today, this was it. It made her want to crawl into that massive bed, pull the covers over her head and sleep until she could wake up in her own narrow bed, in her own two-and-a-half-room apartment with the wag-tailed clock in the kitchen and the fake Oriental rug in the tiny living room.

However, that wasn't possible, and Molly was nothing if not a realist. She surveyed the huge, gleaming bathtub. Her apartment held only a cramped shower. The tub in the only cottage Annamarie had been able to rent on short notice was small, rust stained and uncomfortable, the hot-water supply barely adequate. The hotel's water heater was probably the size of a city block.

Besides, there was that lovely basket of toiletries, just waiting to be sampled. And while she might lack sophistication, she had never been short of common sense.

When Rafe called through the door some twenty minutes later, wanting to know if she was all right, Molly could hardly find the energy to answer. Up to her shoulders in scented bubbles, her hair wet, smelling of passionflower and dewberry bodywash, she seriously considered spending the night right where she was. The water was growing cool, though, and what little energy she possessed had gone flat, along with the bubbles. "I'm fine, thank you," she called back, her voice sounding as drowsy as her boneless body felt.

"Good. We need to talk about tomorrow," came the brisk response.

Molly didn't want to talk about tomorrow. She didn't want to *think* about tomorrow. All her life she'd had to think about tomorrow. Just this once she would like to wallow in a cocoon of luxury and think of nothing more serious than whether or not she should polish her toenails.

"We'll talk tomorrow," she called through the door.

Silence. She could picture him standing on the other side of the door, frustrated and unable to do anything about it. It gave her an exhilarating sense of power.

"Are you sure you're all right in there?" His voice was mild, even concerned. "You're not feeling sick, are you? That pie was pretty rich."

Oh, great. She really needed that. Her eyes suddenly started to sting and she blamed it on the highly scented shampoo. "Would you mind calling the hospital to see if Annamarie's thought of anything else she needs?"

In other words, go away and leave me alone with my sweet-scented guilt and my busted bubbles.

"It's too late to call tonight. You need to go to bed, Molly. We got a heavy schedule tomorrow."

"Stop trying to plan my life. I don't want it and I don't need it. I told you—" She broke off with an indignant yelp as the door opened. It had never occurred to her to lock it. What was the point of having two bathrooms if you couldn't count on a little privacy?

He opened the door and flinched as heavily scented steam surrounded him. "God, you need gills to breathe in here." Holding out an enormous bath towel, he said, "Come on, honey. Time to get out before you turn into a prune."

"Do you *mind?*"

Indignation was hard to hang on to when a woman was sopping wet, bone tired and fighting tears. Add to that about ten thousand calories worth of guilt....

"Get out of the bathtub, Molly."

"Get out of my bathroom, Rafe," she snapped back, but her voice lacked conviction.

"Come on now. You're bound to be bushed. We won't talk about tomorrow's schedule until after we've both had a good night's sleep, if you'd rather not. I left a wake-up call for seven."

Using her toe, she opened the drain. Iridescent bubbles clung to her breasts as the water slowly drained from the tub. Rafe stood patiently, holding the towel outspread. "Anytime you're ready, honey."

"I'm not your honey, and believe it or not, I'm perfectly capable of climbing out of a bathtub."

"Humor me. I've got about all I can handle with Stu's busted head and broken hand. I'm not taking any chances on your slipping and breaking your...whatever."

Well, there was that, too. She felt about as steady on her feet as a string of boiled spaghetti. Besides, he had seen it all before. "Then turn off the light."

"No way. Want me to tell you what I see?"

"Don't you dare," she wailed. "And don't look!"

"I see a wet, beautiful woman with skin like vanilla ice cream. I see a woman whose—"

She lunged into the towel and his arms closed around her. "And I see a man who swallowed the whole blooming Blarney stone," she growled. "Vanilla ice cream?"

"French vanilla. Cream and sugar and—" He sniffed her shoulder. "Maybe a few exotic fruits and flowers."

She choked back a laugh that ended with a sob. "It's passionflower. And dewberries."

"See? I knew it was edible."

Her eyes were still burning from the shampoo, but she had to laugh. When Rafe would have held her there, she pulled away and, still clutching the towel, reached for another one, draping it over her head, face and all. She managed to escape into the bedroom without blundering into any furniture. "All right, you saved me from drowning. Now go away."

"Make me," he purred, grinning.

The towel still covered her head. How on earth did she manage to get herself into these ludicrous situations, one right after the other? Why would any intelligent, levelheaded woman marry a third-rate hustler? Why would she allow herself to be picked up by a sexy-looking fisherman she happened to meet on a ferryboat? Why on earth would she then fall head over heels in love with the very next man she met?

There was no hope for her, simply no hope. During the years when she should have been learning about boy-girl relationships, she'd been too busy pretending to be grown-up so that she could hold her family together. By the time she was free to be herself, it was too late. Ignoring the deficiencies in her social development, she had made one blind leap for the brass ring and missed, and now she was scared stiff of jumping again for fear of breaking something irreparable.

He was still there. She could feel his presence, even though she couldn't see him. Shoving the towel off her face, Molly gave up trying to ignore him. "Scoundrel," she muttered. Clutching the bath towel around her torso, she padded across to the luggage rack. While Rafe stood in the doorway and watched, arms crossed over his chest, she dug out her pajamas. Short of a suit of armor, it was the best she could do. There was certainly nothing seductive about yellow flannel and stringy wet hair. "Would you please leave, or do I have to call for help?"

"Come on out as soon as you're ready. I made fresh coffee."

"You told me I needed sleep. You said we'd wait until morning to talk about what had to be done."

"I lied. I'll give you a choice, though—go to bed, turn off the light, and if you're snoring within five minutes, I'll leave you alone. But if you're planning on lying there in the dark, fretting about how four people are going to fit into a five-room cottage, or how we're all going to get there, then you might as well join me in a nightcap while we go over a plan of operations."

Molly sighed. Under cover of the damp bath towel she had managed to pull on her pajama pants, tug them up and tie the drawstring, thankful the waist was adjustable. She couldn't think of anything more embarrassing than eating an enormous meal and then not being able to get into her clothes.

Tomorrow. Absolutely, without fail tomorrow she would start on the diet of her life, with no time-outs, no excuses, no chocolate rewards for losing two pounds that caused her to gain three more. Not one single forbidden bite until she had lost fifteen pounds. It wasn't enough, but it was a start. At Mary Etta's statuesque five-foot-ten, fifteen extra pounds would hardly even be noticeable, but at five-foot two, those pounds made the difference between the upper-end of average for a large-framed woman—which she wasn't—and overweight. All the charts said so. Charts might lie, but Molly's mirror didn't. Nor had Kenny. For a guy who poured on the smarmy charm like maple syrup when it suited his purpose, her ex-husband knew just how to boost his own ego by slicing hers up into small, bleeding bits. Dumbo had been one of his kinder pet names.

"Black, with one sweetener, right?"

She sighed and buttoned her pajama top up under her chin. "One cup of coffee and that's it. We can talk until I finish, but then I'm going to bed."

After he left the room, she used the hotel's hair dryer for a few minutes, but her hair was too thick and she gave up halfway though. She'd been exhausted before the long, hot soak. Now she felt like a flower-scented zombie. Back when she'd been working two jobs, plus a third on weekends, she'd been younger. Now, at thirty-six, she felt old as the West Virginia hills.

When she came into the lounge, Rafe handed her a thin, gold-banded cup and saucer. "I'll be on the phone first thing tomorrow with the insurance people and the DMV. Then I want to check the car ads in the morning paper. While I do that, why don't you take the rental and go shopping? There's a mall not far away—we passed it on the way to the hotel earlier, remember?''

The thought of trying to find her way around a strange city was daunting, however Molly had tackled worst things in her life. "Fine. Have you got a list for your brother? You'd better specify brands and sizes, because I don't know all that much about men's clothes." Molly shopped at discount stores. Kenny had insisted on buying his things from the most expensive men's store in Morgantown, or ordering from those fancy catalogs that sold battered milking stools for hundreds of dollars and priced faded cotton as if it were woven gold.

She sipped her coffee, hoping the caffeine would kick in while they discussed plans for tomorrow. "We should be able to get the basics out of the way by about ten," Rafe said. "I'll meet you back here when you're through shopping and we'll run out to the hospital and see if we can bail the honeymooners out. After that we'll grab some lunch and then leave them here while you and I check out the car dealers."

Molly nodded silently. She knew what it was like to be broke. She couldn't imagine what it must be like to have lost everything, right down to driver's license and Social Security card. Some things could not be replaced at the corner drugstore. "Won't Stu want to pick out his own car?"

"He trusts me."

Leaning back in her chair Molly tucked her bare feet up beside her and studied the man across from her. Mercy, he was beautiful. That sun-streaked hair hadn't come from any bottle, any more than that spectacular tan had. Molly had belatedly developed an excellent instinct for phonies, and whatever else he was, Rafe was no phony—he was genuine to the bone. You could take him or leave him; he couldn't care less. Everything about him practically shouted that message.

And Molly would have given her last earthly possession to take him, but that wasn't a choice she'd been offered, except on a strictly temporary basis. Once Stu and Annamarie were settled, Rafe would go back to the lifestyle of the rich and famous and she would go back to the lifestyle of a head-housekeeper at Holly Hills Home.

"Isn't that right?"

"Isn't what right?"

"Wake up, darling. You haven't heard a thing I've said for the past five minutes, have you?"

"I warned you I wasn't up to a serious planning session tonight."

"You did." He stood and held out his hand. Molly sighed and took it, but only because she honestly didn't think she possessed the strength to resist. He tugged her to her feet and then held her in a loose embrace, his chin resting on the top of her head. "Molly, Molly, what am I going to do about you?" he murmured, his voice almost too soft to be heard over the clumsy thump-ka-thud of her heart.

"I don't know," she said simply. Hopefully. Hopelessly.

"I know what I'd like to do, but let's get this other business sorted out first."

Rafe had been asleep for about three hours. There'd been a time when he could go without sleep for thirty-six hours without losing his edge. Now it was more like twenty-four. He could still fall asleep within minutes, catnap and wake up fresh and ready to meet trouble head on, but he rarely slept so deeply that the slightest sound didn't bring him instantly alert.

He was instantly alert. Silently he slipped out of bed and felt for his khakis. By the time he reached Molly's bedroom door, he was marginally decent. He listened, not knowing what he was listening for, but knowing he would recognize it if it came again.

Thump! The sound of muffled curses. He opened the door a crack and peered into the darkness, wondering how good hotel security was, wishing he had brought along his own protection. Even four star hotels had their share of break-ins.

"Oh, dammit, dammit, dammit." Molly's voice. She sounded as if she were in pain, but not as if she were fighting off an intruder. He'd been in enough tight situations to recognize the difference.

Reaching inside the door, he switched on the entry light, all sixty watts of it. She was sitting on the floor clutching one foot, rocking back and forth and muttering, "Dammit, dammit, dammit" in a dull monotone. Stifling the urge to laugh, he entered, leaving the door open. "Got a problem?"

"My toe—or rather, my leg and my toe." And then she uttered a basic four letter word that was so un-Molly-like he had to laugh.

Kneeling before her, he took her foot into his own hands. "Let me guess. Another blister? You got up to go to the bathroom and stubbed your toe?"

"I got a leg cramp and got up to walk it off and tripped over that—that damn-blasted chair!" She glared at the guilty chair, but as Rafe began to massage her calf and the small, childlike foot, she sighed

and closed her eyes. "I can do that myself. I was
getting ready to."

"Hush up and let my magic fingers go to work.
Your arms are too short, remember?" He was sitting
cross-legged on the floor in front of her, beside the
bed. The covers were spilling onto the floor, as if the
bed itself had been under attack.

"This is getting to be an embarrassing habit," she
muttered. "You and my feet."

"You need to take better care of yourself. Is this
better?"

"I take excellent care of myself. I always have."

"Right," he said with a knowing look as he gently
manipulated the spasming muscles at the back of her
leg.

She flinched when he touched a trigger spot, and
Rafe smoothed the place with long, slow strokes,
watching her mouth tense, then soften. Watching the
way her gold-tipped russet eyelashes curled on her
cheek when her eyes were closed. After a while she
said, "I always walk. Even when I'm tied to my desk
all day, I always walk at least a couple of miles. Today I didn't."

"Mmm." There was the faintest dusting of fine,
transparent hair on her lower legs, none at all above
the knee. She didn't shave, and for some reason, that
struck him as incredibly arousing. No polish on her
toenails. She was pure, plain Molly. What you saw
was what you got.

He very much liked what he saw. And what he felt.
And the heady scent of warm, sleepy woman with
overtones of some fruity-scented body lotion. Liked
it too much...and that was beginning to be a problem.

The trouble with Molly was that she was nothing

at all like the women who had left their mark on his life to a greater or lesser degree, starting with his mother, a Vegas showgirl. Gorgeous even somewhere in her early sixties, Stella loved romance with a capital *R*. She had married often and loved every one of her husbands, but if she'd ever had a maternal bone in her body, it had yet to be discovered.

Molly was purring, her eyes almost closed, but not quite. Funny thing about women. His ex-wife, eighteen at the time they were married, had never liked being touched. He hadn't seen her—had scarcely even thought about her in the sixteen years since their divorce. But he could still remember how he'd felt when she'd announced shortly after their wedding that she would do the Dirty Deed with him whenever he required her to, but she preferred to sleep alone.

At the time he'd been as hormone-driven as any normal nineteen-year-old. Once he realized she meant it, he'd told her she was flat-out crazy. With nothing else to sustain it, their brief marriage had gone downhill from there. It had been years before he'd trusted his judgment with any woman. Even now, he never asked for more than he was prepared to offer, which definitely ruled out any emotional involvement.

Until Molly.

Over the years, he'd run pretty true to type where women were concerned. Invariably he was drawn to brunettes. One of the sexiest women he'd ever known had a sleek cap of blue-black hair and almond-shaped eyes the color of green seedless grapes. Molly's hair was long, reddish brown and inclined to curl. Her eyes were as round and brown as chestnuts.

He'd always been turned on by tall women, athletic types with long legs, lean bodies and small breasts.

Molly was short and well-rounded, generously endowed in every area.

The one thing that was nonnegotiable in the women he guardedly allowed into his life was detachment. No clinging vines. No demands on either side. The only reason he had broken off with Belle, who fit all his requirements to a T, was that, approaching the age of forty she had discovered a long-buried nesting urge.

Molly dropped off the charts in every single category. A woman who had helped raise two sisters? No way. She was one of those women whatsername sang about—people who needed people. If she'd struck out on her own after her folks had been killed, leaving her sisters with other relatives, it might be different, but she wasn't the type to shirk her responsibilities.

Right. Like you didn't take on the care and feeding of a fifteen-year-old kid when you were barely making it yourself.

Okay, so they both had a few weaknesses. All the more reason not to get any more involved than they already were, Rafe told himself.

"Your hands have got to be tired. I'm all right now, honestly. See?" She wiggled her toes. Small, straight toes with nails as pink as the inside of a conch shell.

"You sure? You've got a long list tomorrow."

"Just move that blasted chair on your way out, will you?"

Rafe was grateful for the dim lighting. It didn't take much candlepower to recognize temptation when it was lying back, propped back on a pair of dimpled elbows with one knee bent, one leg resting across his lap. Those flannel pajamas of hers, with the rabbit-print collar and cuffs, were definitely not one of Victoria's secrets. He started to ease her foot onto the floor. She sighed. He slid his hands to the back of her knee and heard her catch her breath.

"You're ticklish," he accused.

"Only when you touch me behind the knees," she gasped.

Well, naturally, he had to test her.

One thing led to another—later, the only conclusion he could draw was that they both wanted what followed. His fingers traced the dimples at the back of her knee and she planted her stubby little foot on his chest and shoved. Like a kid—like a feisty ten-year-old kid. He retaliated by rolling over her and tickling her ribs.

One thing led to another. The bedding was half on the floor by then. So he dragged it the rest of the way. Making love to a woman on even the best grade of commercial carpet simply wasn't his style, and he knew what was going to happen. At some level, he'd known it when he'd opened her door.

Ten

Fingering the soft, rumpled fabric of her pajama top, Rafe said, "Is this what you always sleep in?"

"Yes—no—sometimes."

"I like a woman who knows her own mind."

The pajama top came unbuttoned as if by magic. Molly had a stern mental talk with herself about the advisability of deliberately courting disaster. It lasted all of thirty seconds. She tried to tell herself she couldn't possibly be in love with the man, not after less than a week, but it felt more like love than anything she had ever before experienced. Even at the very first, when she'd been suspicious of him and tried to talk him into leaving, it was as if she had recognized him at some deep, subconscious level. If only he had recognized her in the same way....

Still, she would have this much, no matter what. This time they were equal partners. The same wild magic that had propelled them headlong into ecstasy the first time they had made love prevailed once more, but now there was the added element of tenderness. The feeling that this would be a farewell gift made her want to weep.

Lifting his mouth from her breast, Rafe moved down her body. "Let me—" he whispered hoarsely.

"Oh, please—you can't," she said as shivers of sheer pleasure raced though her boneless body.

He could, and he did, and long moments later, Molly cried out her pleasure. Then, with the coals of passion still glowing, he came into her and they rocked together, holding on tightly, murmuring soft broken words until they succumbed to an avalanche of sheer, mindless sensation.

Rafe watched her guardedly the following morning. She wouldn't meet his eyes, but he could feel her gaze focus on him the moment he turned away. There was a sense of sadness about her that didn't make sense. God knows, the last thing he wanted was to have her regret what had happened. Briefly he considered bringing it up—cards on the table, so to speak—but sex was something he'd never felt comfortable discussing. Especially when he was still feeling off balance. He couldn't put his finger on what it was; he only knew that some vital element in his life had changed.

Before he thought too deeply about it—if he had to think about it at all—he preferred to put some distance between them. About a thousand miles should put things in perspective. "How're your leg cramps?"

She looked for a moment as if he'd tossed her a

live mouse. Then, ignoring his question, she picked up her list and read off, "Two sets of clothes, under and outer, for both. Toothbrushes, toothpaste, deodorant, moisturizer—Annamarie doesn't need much makeup. Do you know what Stu needs for shaving? Brands and everything? And they'll need pens and a notepad to list things as they think of them and…whatever."

Rafe named a well-known brand of shaving cream and suggested a pack of disposable razors. "Stu had his wallet on him. Your sister lost her purse, so that'll mean a new drivers' license, new Social Security card—"

"New library card."

"Oh, yeah, can't forget library card," he said dryly, and that brought a smile to her lips. It felt as if the sun had just come blazing out after a three-day hurricane.

By the time they finished breakfast they had allocated duties. Molly went over her lists while Rafe scribbled notes on the hotel stationery and waited impatiently for the insurance office to open. Neither of them mentioned the night before, but it hovered like a third presence in the room. They avoided looking directly at each other, avoided mentioning anything even faintly personal.

Molly was all efficiency, dressing quickly in her black top and jeans. She was down to her last clean outfit. Thank goodness the waistband wasn't too tight today. Occasionally she played games with herself, telling herself it was only water weight, but weight was weight. Measurements were measurements. And Molly was nothing if not a realist.

Thanks to her new pomegranate-pink lipstick and

a touch of blusher, the shadows beneath her eyes weren't so noticeable. Glancing at her watch, she said, "The stores should be open now. I want to allow enough time to find the mall—I think it's on this same street, about two or three blocks south. Or was it north?"

Rafe pointed toward a colorful serigraph on the wall beside the door. "Which direction is that?"

Molly blinked. "Out?"

He shook his head. "Just ask directions from the concierge."

"The what?"

"It's a who. Lady in the lobby, behind the stand-alone desk with the big, potted anthurium."

She scowled at him. "I knew that," she said when it was plain as day that she'd known nothing of the kind.

Which might have been what prompted Rafe to cross the floor just as she reached for her purse, take her in his arms and kiss her on the mouth. It was a soft kiss, not at all passionate, yet all the more devastating for that. Because there was that tenderness again. Passion was one thing, she told herself—passion could flare up for purely chemical reasons and burn itself out within minutes.

Tenderness had a way of lingering long after the flames had died down.

He pressed the car keys and several large bills in her hand and said, "Go shopping. If this doesn't cover it, we'll go back later. Meet you back here about noon."

Rafe talked to the insurance agent and got the ball rolling. He had looked at several cars. "Something a damned sight safer than that high-priced cookie tin you were driving,'' was the criterion he described to Stu when he'd called to discuss the matter. After that, he spent a few hours on the phone, most of them on hold, with various offices and agencies.

With a list of sizes, styles and brands, Molly shopped diligently. Stu was easy. Boxers, white socks and clunky sneakers, size ten medium. As long as his clothes fit, he was happy. If he had an ego, it wasn't based on his appearance.

Annamarie was a bit more demanding, but as she'd look gorgeous wearing kitchen curtains, Molly had bought her underwear, two pairs of dark slacks and two pretty tops, sandals and sneakers. Pajamas for both, plus the toiletries, plus two bags of M&Ms. Annamarie would need her favorite comfort food.

Just as they finished comparing notes over the sandwiches Rafe had ordered from room service, Stu called to say he'd already been discharged, but Annamarie was undergoing tests to be sure the recurring pain in her side was nothing more than a strained muscle.

Hearing that, Molly started fidgeting. And then she started listing every known internal injury and a few no one had ever heard of.

''A strained goozle?'' Rafe glanced up from his own lists.

''Oh, it's the—you know. The whatchamacallit. I knew a boy who fell off a tractor and they had to take it out, but he got along just fine without it. But it might be— Oh, Lordy, what if they can't have children? That would break her heart.''

''Molly. Look at me. Close your eyes. Take a deep breath and listen. You're probably talking about a spleen. It has nothing to do with having children. If it has to go, she can live without it. Besides, the tests are only a precaution. If there's the slightest chance of a liability suit, the hospital's not going to let her walk out without the appropriate tests.''

Eyes closed, she said, ''I need to be there. She'll need me.''

''She has a husband now. How about letting him take over the responsibility?''

She opened her eyes and looked at him then, really looked at him for the first time since they'd made love. Golden brown eyes, dark now with apprehension. It was all he could do not to reach for her, but it was time to pull back. Time to begin erecting barriers again. ''Trust me,'' Rafe said, and she nodded.

''You're right. I'm just—it's habit, I guess. I told you Mama wasn't exactly—that is, she was always so tired. She worked—did I tell you that? But she still found time to make most of our clothes and teach me to sew when I was growing up.''

''Mine taught me dance routines. Can't tell you what a big help those high kicks were once I started playing football.''

Molly had to laugh. He shook his head—she thought he might have said something under his breath, but then he was holding her, and there was nothing at all sexual about it, only caring. Come to think about it, that was even more terrifying than the other. The knowledge that she cared too much. And that while he might care just a little bit, too, when it came to caring, there was no middle ground. Too much on one side and not enough on the other could never add up to happiness.

* * *

Rafe was not the classic loner. He had scores of friends. He had known hundreds of women and enjoyed dozens of them intimately. He'd always considered himself a generous man, both as a friend and a lover.

But deep down, where it counted, he had always held a part of himself aloof. Only once had he broken the rule, and then it was for a lonely, klutzy, resentful kid with a redwood-size chip on his shoulder. Stu had tried his damnedest to prove something to the big brother he'd been dumped on, to the mother who had done the dumping, and to the father who hadn't bothered to see him since he was about four years old. For the first couple of years he'd nearly broken his neck trying to become something he was never cut out to be. Rafe had realized one thing from his own youth—telling a kid didn't work. Keeping him alive while he learned who he was, what he was all about and where his capabilities lay, turned out to be a large order, but somebody had to tackle it. What the hell could a big brother do but love him, try to teach him a few survival skills and keep him out of major trouble?

Now he had a wife. He was no longer lonely or resentful. He might still be something of a klutz, but he was Annamarie's klutz. Neither of them would appreciate Rafe's stepping in and trying to run the show.

Rafe called the hospital room to describe the SUV he had picked out. Annamarie answered and said Stu had gone out to get her something in chocolate, preferably M&Ms. "We've decided on a pickup truck. It's a lot more practical and just as safe."

Rafe figured Annamarie had decided. Stu's inter-

ests ran more to Roman chariots than to modern transportation. "Okay, your call. How about dark green?"

"Orange. You can see it coming from a mile
away."

"I don't think pickup trucks come in orange."

"Maybe not, but paint does."

On the whole, Rafe decided as he hung up with
plans to collect Stu after visiting hours, he liked his
new sister-in-law.

He also liked his sister-in-law's sister, he thought
late that afternoon as he went through the preflight
checkup. And that might be something of a problem.

Summer had struck with a vengeance. Five in the
afternoon on the first day of May, with the temperature hovering in the eighties. Molly was wearing a
new pair of dark pants which hugged her shapely
hips, with a white open-throated cotton shirt. A plain
white shirt that looked sexier than another woman's
thong bikini. Imagination was a hell of an aphrodi-
siac.

Mayday, mayday!

Silently she climbed in and strapped herself down
without speaking a word. She'd hardly spoken on the
way to the airport. She was worrying again. Not about
money, because Stu still had his credit cards. It would
take more than a bottom-of-the-line pickup truck to
max out his credit. They'd bought the truck—it was
red, not orange—and Annamarie would be driving
until Stu's hand healed.

She was probably worried about her sister's driving. Hadn't she mentioned something about the trouble Annamarie had had getting her driver's license?
"Look, they're going to be cautious as the devil after
what happened. I wouldn't worry."

And then he remembered that her parents had gone off a mountain road in a hard rainstorm and both been killed. "Great roads between Norfolk and Ocracoke. Straight, wide, flat. Not a lot of traffic this time of year." He didn't have a clue about the traffic—Memorial Day was coming up—but it was what she needed to hear.

"I know," she said almost too softly to be heard. "And thank you, Rafe. For—well, for everything."

As they lifted off the runway, he concentrated on flying. Not until they reached cruising altitude did he respond. "I'm not sure what everything you're talking about, but you're certainly welcome." He'd given Stu most of the cash he had on him and paid for another night at the hotel, figuring it wouldn't be a bad idea for the younger adults to be within range of medical care for a day or so before heading back. He wasn't sure about the medical facilities on the island.

"I hope the birds haven't taught Carly too many bad words." Molly had been watching the patterns pass below. The geometric patchwork of fields and doll-size farms, and then the lacework of sounds and creeks, rivers and ponds as they neared the coast.

"I wouldn't be surprised if she hasn't taught them a few."

She looked at him then. "Rafe, she's only a child."

"Yeah," he said, and she shook her head and then laughed. For the first time all day—since they had made love, in fact, she seemed visibly to relax. They hadn't slept together last night. Stu, dismissed from the hospital, had shared Rafe's room, then insisted on racing off to the hospital to spring his wife. It had taken a couple of hours, after which they had gone to the dealer's to collect the new truck.

He had a feeling Molly had spent the most of the time while he was gone making a list of every penny he'd spent on her so that she could settle her account. When he'd come back, she'd been on the phone with her other sister—Etta Mary or was it Mary Etta? There was a stack of receipts and several pages of hotel stationary on the desk beside her.

He'd listened in unabashedly while he poured himself a big glass of orange juice from the minirefrigerator. Molly had obviously explained what had happened, and how it was being dealt with, and was in the process of explaining why she'd been free to house-sit while Annamarie was off on a birthday-gift trip with her new husband.

Rafe had already known most of it. He'd learned about two of the three sisters from watching the interaction between Molly and Annamarie at the hospital. For all their apparent differences, they were surprisingly close. They finished each other's sentences. Molly would say, "Remember that time—"

"—when I dressed Miss Daisy's cat up in doll clothes and it got away?"

And then they would laugh, and Annamarie would say, "If it had been anybody else she would have—"

"The finger. She had the biggest forefinger I ever saw," Molly had explained to Stu and Rafe. "She was always shaking it in someone's face, like it was a—"

"—a weapon. When you're only about three feet tall, and—"

"And there's this huge forefinger shaking right in your face, believe me, it makes a big—"

"—impression, even when you know she'd never lay a hand on you." Annamarie had grinned without diminishing the china-doll perfection of her face. "She might have taken a switch to me, but she would never in this world have hurt you." And to Rafe she'd explained, "Everybody loves Molly."

"Annamarie, that's not—"

"Oh, yes it is. There's not a man, woman or child in all of Grover's Hollow who hasn't—"

"For heaven's sake, you're boring everyone to death!" Molly's cheeks were flaming.

"Well, anyway, they all love her," the younger sister had insisted. Barefooted, wearing a hospital gown over a pair of pink plaid slacks, she'd looked all of twelve years old as she proceeded to embarrass and defend her older sister at the same time.

Rafe had listened with half an ear, trying to bring into focus a younger Molly who had helped to raise both her sisters. A woman whose taste in men was on a par with her taste in seashells, collecting broken specimens of both. A woman who was surprisingly naive, considering she had been married and divorced.

And now that her sisters were out on their own, Rafe thought now as he followed the coastline on a southwesterly course, she was probably going to hole up in some retirement home and spend the rest of her life looking after people who would take advantage of her sweet, generous spirit until she was all used up. No more blushes. No more laughter. No more fresh, dewy cheeks and soft sighs and uninhibited passion.

It was a damned shame, too. Not that there was a sentimental bone in his entire body, but a woman like Molly would bring out the protective instincts of a totem pole. What she needed was—

Was none of his business!

* * *

"I guess they'll be here sometime tomorrow,"
Molly said brightly a few hours later. She had a kink
in her neck from watching a spectacular sunset over
the broad waters of the Pamlico Sound. They had
barely made it back to the island before dark. Rafe
had mentioned that there were no lights on the runway and then concentrated on flying, although from
time to time she felt his gaze on her. They hadn't
tried to talk over the engine noise, and for that Molly
was grateful.

Now she swung herself down from the plane without waiting for his help. No point in getting used to
something that was about to end. After today, the pets
would no longer need her. The cottage was barely big
enough for a couple of honeymooners. Four was definitely a crowd.

"I guess you'll be leaving in the morning," she
said with every appearance of cheerfulness.

He nodded. "I told Stu not to be in too big a hurry,
in case your sister needs more—more time to shop."
Rafe had been about to say, more medical attention,
but Molly was a world-class worrier.

"She won't. She has clothes here, and more back
in Durham."

"But as long as they're near the shops, she might
want to indulge."

"She'll be fine with what I bought her. I know her
tastes and her sizes."

Personally Rafe had never known a woman, including his own mother, who wasn't a marathon
shopper. The more beautiful they were, the more they
enjoyed spending his money to enhance that beauty.

All his mistresses had been high-maintenance types. "At any rate, Stu can afford it. He won't come into his trust until he's thirty-one, but he has an interest income that should keep her happy until then."

Molly gave him a curious look. With the plane secured, they were in the rust bucket, headed back to the cottage. "Is that what it takes to be happy? Money?"

"Doesn't it?" It was like having a sensitive tooth. He couldn't leave it alone, he had to keep probing, testing, ferreting out weaknesses in order not to fall any deeper under her spell. He told himself it was only the novelty factor. That's all it could be, because Molly was different in every conceivable way from his usual women.

Under the low branches of two twisted live oak trees, the cottage was dark. Rafe unlocked the door and Molly stepped inside and felt for the light switch. Pete—or was it Repete?—tuned up with the squeaking door imitation, and the other bird made a chattering noise that sounded like a scolding wren. Actually, Molly thought, they were rather nice birds as long as they weren't spouting profanity.

So, of course they had to start. Every indecent four-letter word known to man. Someone—probably the entire fraternity—had taken great delight in corrupting a pair of otherwise beautiful birds.

"It's a wonder they don't blister the paint," Rafe observed.

"*Bugger off, mate, bugger off, mate, bu—*"

"*Bad-ass, bad-ass!*"

"They don't seem to bother your sister."

"Actually they do, but nobody else would claim

them and she was afraid they'd be—well, whatever you do to unwanted birds. Euthanize them, I guess.''

Rafe dropped the bags in the two bedrooms, opened windows and then peered into the refrigerator. ''They're probably long past frying age, but stewed, they might be—''

''Rafe!''

''Only kidding,'' he said. ''Want a... Let's see, we could have a bacon-and-cheese omelet or—''

Hearing Shag at the door, Molly opened a can of cat food. No wonder the poor creature always stunk. So did his dinner. ''Sally Ann wants me take a puppy.''

''So?'' Rafe got out the ingredients for an omelet and lined them up on the counter.

''The place where I live has a no-pets policy.''

''Call it a guard dog.''

''I could call it a stuffed duck, but I don't think it would work.''

Molly was almost too tired to eat. She couldn't think why, as she'd done little but sit for the past few hours, conscious every minute of the man beside her—his warmth, his strength, the woody scent of his shaving soap mingling with the oil-and-metal smell of the plane itself. ''You wouldn't think you could get tired of resting, would you?''

Rafe was whipping eggs. Oddly enough, there was nothing at all incongruous about a large, rugged man wearing tailor-made khakis and a stylish chambray shirt with a flowered tea towel tucked under his belt.

''I'd better get to work, too,'' Molly said, and jumped up so fast, her head swam. Then she stood there like a fool, not knowing where to start, what to

do. "They'll probably be here sometime tomorrow. I
should clean the house."

"Why? Did they clean up before you came?"

"That's different."

"How is it different?"

"I don't know!" she cried, flinging out her arms
helplessly. "It just is! I've always cleaned when company was coming. It's—it's expected."

The bacon was sizzling on the back burner. Rafe
poured the egg mixture into the omelet pan and let it
set before he began tilting and lifting. Calmly he said,
"Sit down, Molly. They won't be here until tomorrow
evening at the earliest. You need to eat a good supper
and go to bed. In the morning you can start worrying
again. If necessary, I'll help you with a list of things
to worry about."

She had to laugh. It was the strangest thing, but
when it occurred to her that he was saying exactly
the same sort of thing to her that she'd said for years
to Annamarie and Mary Etta, laughter bubbled up inside her like antacid tablets dropped in water.

"What, you think that's funny? You want to get
started on tomorrow's list now? How about the Middle East situation? Those earthquakes? The price of
oil and what it's doing to the economy?"

And then she howled. "I want extra cheese in
mine," she said when she could speak again.

"Hmm...it's sort of green," he warned. "I'd better
shave off the mold."

"Who cares? I'll put mold on the list of things to
worry about tomorrow."

She would worry about more than moldy cheese
tomorrow, but meanwhile she intended to enjoy what
might be the last few hours she would ever have with

the man who had opened her eyes to what love was all about.

It was about laughing together. About sharing. About fitting together body, soul and mind, as if they were two parts of a whole. It was about that scary, thrilling feeling of knowing that for better or worse you're connected in some mysterious way to another being and there's not one blooming thing you can do about it.

And when the worst came, letting go.

Rafe hadn't exactly said when he was leaving, but it would probably be shortly after Stu and Annamarie got here tomorrow. He'd mentioned waiting to see that they got here safely, but after that, if there was enough light left to fly by, there'd be no more reason for him to hang around.

She might even leave before he did, just to prove she could walk away. Meanwhile she had tonight.

By the time she'd finished her half of the omelet and two glasses of wine, she was having trouble holding her eyes open. "That was delicious, but I can't seem to stop yawning. Would you mind if I wait until morning to do the dishes?"

She hadn't made the bed before they'd left. Now she barely managed to peel off her clothes and drag on her pajama top. Tomorrow she would get busy sweeping and dusting and worrying about the rest of her life and how she was going to fill a big hole in her heart.

Maybe Stu and Annamarie would have babies.

Maybe…

Eleven

Hearing Rafe in the shower, Molly stared up at the water-stained ceiling and went over her mental worry list again. Annamarie would be all right; she had Stu now. And Stu had had Rafe for a role model, so how could he possibly not do well? Which brought her back around to the top of the list.

How about Molly? How was she going to keep from bleeding to death when she watched him drive off in that noisy old rust bucket? Or when she watched him fly off in that shiny white plane with the green palm tree and the orange sunset? Could she shrug it off, pretending it didn't matter?

It wasn't as if he had promised her anything, or even asked for anything. She would willingly have given him her heart, but then, why would he want a heart that had another man's footprints all over it?

Babies, she decided, would be a link. He'd be the

uncle, she the aunt. There would be holidays, family reunions—those were real big occasions back in Grover's Hollow. Maybe not so big in Pelican's Cove, but then, it was something to look forward to, which was a whole lot better than nothing.

Outside the open window a mockingbird tuned up and ran through an impressive repertoire. It occurred to her that before the summer was over, the same bird might be showing off an X-rated vocabulary. Maybe she would think about that possibility and laugh, rather than think about impossibilities and cry.

"I saved you some hot water," Rafe called through the door. He poked his head inside, his wet hair several shades darker. His eyes were...*veiled* was the only word she could think of to describe the way he looked at her. "Rise and shine, lazy bones. You've got a kitchen full of dirty dishes that have to be washed before I can make us some breakfast."

Funny, Molly thought, how quickly habits could be formed, rituals established. She washed the dishes and then she stripped the beds. And since the sun was shining, she put in a load of wash. The washing machine protested—its innards were probably full of sand—but being busy was the only way she knew to keep from thinking.

She ate two scrambled eggs and drank freshly squeezed orange juice and Rafe's strong Columbian coffee and thought, *This is the last time we'll share breakfast. Stu and Annamarie will be here this afternoon, and Rafe will want to get back to whatever he left down in Florida.*

Or whoever.

"I'm going to the store. Do you want to come with

me?'' he said, raking his chair back and glancing at his watch.

Even his voice set off her internal seismograph. ''No, you go ahead. I need to hang out the wash.'' They had discussed it yesterday and decided to clean out their leftovers from the refrigerator and restock it with easy meal makings. With one hand in a cast, Stu wouldn't be a whole lot of help for a week or so, and Annamarie had never been particularly domestic.

Through the front window, Molly watched Rafe drive off. She tried to tell herself she was allergic to salt air, but it wasn't salt air that was making her throat ache and her eyes brim over. Maybe it wasn't love—she'd been fooled before—but whatever it was, right now it hurt like the very devil, and she had to start getting over it. No way was she going to waste the rest of her life moping over a man who was probably down in Florida feeding some skinny little bimbo in a string bikini his Irish coffee and sweet potato casserole.

''Balderdash,'' she muttered.

She hung the wash, including two of Rafe's shirts, a pair of khakis and two pairs of briefs, and thought with a wicked sense of satisfaction, *He can't pack up and leave until his laundry dries or it'll mildew.*

Glancing at the sun, feeling the southwest breeze on her face, she felt her spirits droop. So maybe she would simply leave before he did. Dressed in her black skirt and turtleneck. Of course, it would be too hot because today promised to be a scorcher, but it was by far her most flattering outfit. She could drape a scarf over her shoulder so that it would flutter in the breeze as she walked away. Not looking back, leaving behind only a taunting whiff of Je Reviens, which the clerk had told her meant something like "I'm coming back" in French. Would that be subtle enough? Too subtle? Would he even notice?

Go now, and don't look back. She'd heard that clichéd line all her life, and hadn't a clue where it came from, but suddenly it didn't seem all that melodramatic.

"I stocked up on deli stuff and a frozen pumpkin pie," Rafe told her as he unloaded the rust bucket. She was in the yard taking in the sheets, which had dried, and feeling her jeans, which would never dry. He'd almost caught her testing his briefs, which were dry except for the elastic.

He handed her a plastic sack. "Brought you a gift, something to remember me by," he said with that grin of his that ought to be labeled as hazardous to a woman's health.

He'd brought her a bright orange plastic raincoat and matching hat. "Lose the beige," he said.

She didn't know whether to laugh or cry. "I'd planned to. It doesn't shed water anymore." Clutching the plastic raingear to her chest, she tried to think of something to give him in return. Something that would remind him of her when he was back in Florida.

"Think this'll serve as a traveling cage?" He dragged a banana box out of the back of the rust bucket. "It's ventilated."

"A cage? You're taking the birds?"

He frowned, and she thought, I'd rather have one of his frowns than a smile from any other man in the world. "Pups. I thought I might take a couple. If I don't, Stu'll get suckered into taking the whole litter. He's got a weakness for animals—always did have.''

''Well, now we know what they have in common,'' Molly said dryly. ''Annamarie dragged home every stray in Grover's Hollow. Did I ever tell you about the dying pony someone gave her? Mama had a fit, but Annamarie was so sure she could cure the poor thing and learn to ride it. It was her dream back then—to be a cowgirl.''

''I'm afraid to ask what happened.'' Rafe shoved the box onto the porch and took a sack of groceries in each hand.

Molly draped the fresh-smelling sheets over her shoulder and lifted out the last sack. ''I buried the poor thing. And let me tell you, it's not easy digging a pony-size hole in our section of West Virginia. Annamarie nailed together a wooden cross and was about to dig up Mama's rosebush to plant on his grave, but I bribed her with three packets of flower seeds and a trip to the library. You do know the puppies aren't even weaned yet, don't you?''

''They're not? Carly never mentioned it. I guess I'll have to come back in a couple of weeks, whenever they're ready to fly.''

Oh, sure. Once she was gone he could come back any old time and stay as long as he liked. There wasn't a single reason in the world why that should make her feel like an outsider, but it did. ''Are you allowed to keep pets?''

''Yes'm, I'm allowed,'' he replied, and his eyes took on that look of gentle amusement that melted her defensive anger before she could dig herself in any deeper. She had slept with the man, for heaven's sake. She was ninety-nine percent in love with him. So? As Carly would say—get over it!

"That's right. You own the hotels, or whatever, don't you?"

"At the moment, one of them could be described as a 'whatever,' but the Coral Tree Inn is completely renovated and ready to go on the block."

"To sell, you mean. Is that what you do? Sell hotels?"

"Buy 'em, renovate or demolish and rebuild on the property, then sell and start all over again. It's an interesting business."

"I'm sure," she said, trying not to sound the way she was feeling, which was left out in the cold. Miffed.

No, not miffed, dammit, devastated!

Loaded with laundry and groceries, she paused just inside the door. "You'd better put the cold stuff in the refrigerator. I've got beds to make and packing to do." As a romantic, dramatic parting line, it left a lot to be desired, but it was the best she could come up with. Some women just weren't cut out for leading roles in any man's life.

While Molly was remaking the bed and straightening the office, replacing the stacks of books, papers, tapes and recording equipment on the cot Rafe had used when he wasn't sleeping in the other bed with her, Stu called from Oregon Inlet to say they'd be getting in by midafternoon.

Plenty of time to get away before dark, Rafe told himself.

Plenty of time to leave before Rafe did, Molly told herself. Meanwhile she would think of some casual, witty farewell line and practice it until the final moment came.

"I was scared to death driving onto the ferry," Annamarie exclaimed. "But Stu, bless his heart, didn't yell at me a single time. Molly, is that your suitcase by the door?"

Within minutes of their arrival, the cottage Molly had taken such pains to leave spotless was littered with parcels, flyers, folders and books. Neatness was not one of Annamarie's attributes.

"I thought I might try and catch the—"

"Oh, honey, you're an angel to put up with my babies. I know how cursing gets to you, but they don't really curse, they just use—well, actually, most of their words have a perfectly legitimate origin if you go back far enough."

"Spoken like a true linguist," Molly said, laughing. She shook her head. She had filled her gas tank and washed the salt from her windshield earlier. She was all ready to leave, while Rafe was sprawled in the easy chair, seemingly in no hurry to go. It was going to work, if only she could remember what it was she'd meant to say to him. Her casual, unforgettable parting line.

"Golly, aren't you hot in that black outfit?" Annamarie was wearing the blue pants Molly had picked out, with the white camp shirt. She had kicked off her sandals the minute she'd come inside.

"No, I—that is, it's more comfortable for driving than—" She was going to say than tight jeans. Instead she turned to Rafe and said, "It was nice, um— meeting you, Rafe."

Nice meeting him? I can't believe I said that.

"Oh, I expect we'll run into each other sooner or later."

"Your chambray shirt's still damp around the yoke and the cuffs. You'll need to take it out as soon as you get home so it won't mildew."

So much for the memorable parting word. Molly the head housekeeper strikes again.

"Honey, you need to take your pills. The doctor said—" Annamarie glanced up from the sofa, where she was cradling Stu's cast on her lap. "Oh, but you two don't have to leave just because we're back. At least stay for supper. We can go out somewhere."

But it was obvious to both Rafe and Molly that they were superfluous. Rafe spoke for both. "It's already after four, We'd better get going. I promised your next-door neighbor I'd take a couple of her pups when they're weaned, though, so I'll be seeing you before too long."

"And you two will be stopping by Holly Hills to see me on your way back to Durham, won't you?" Molly forced a smile and was reaching for her bag when Rafe took it from her.

"How about following me to the rental place so I can turn in the rust bucket? You can give me a lift to the airport since you'll be passing by on your way to the ferry."

The newlyweds beamed their approval, obviously delighted that their respective relatives were getting along so well together.

If they only knew, thought Molly as she hugged them both goodbye.

"See you in a couple of weeks," Rafe said. He hugged his brother and kissed his new sister on the cheek. Pride fought with jealousy as Molly followed him outside.

"You go on, I'll follow. We'll gas up your car when we drop off the SUV," Rafe said.

"Thanks, but I've already taken care of it." The big payoff. An orange raincoat and a tank full of gas. "Be still my heart," she muttered as she backed out onto the narrow, oyster-shell-paved road.

They drove in silence after Rafe turned in the vehicle and climbed into her passenger seat. Molly tried to think of some way to crowd a lifetime into a few minutes. She tried to remember Ingrid Bergman's parting words in *Casablanca,* but then, she'd been the one who boarded a plane, not Humphrey.

"Well," Rafe said as they pulled into the parking space outside the pavilion. There were three planes left on the tarmac. It was Wednesday. By weekend, there might be a dozen, but his wouldn't be among them.

Nor would Molly be waiting for him.

He thought of a dozen things he could say, all of them clichés. Reaching into the back seat he lifted out his duffel bag and opened the door. "Don't get out. I know you want to be on your way. I understand the ferries run often enough so that if you miss one, there'll be another along pretty soon."

Amber eyes. He could have sworn they were too clear to hide behind, only this time he hadn't a clue what she was thinking. "Guess this is it, then," he said jovially, and could have kicked himself when he saw those eyes darken.

"I guess it is. If I don't see you again—" Molly's smile was too quick, too bright.

Rafe cleared his throat. "Yeah, well…"

Molly wanted to cry, *Kiss me goodbye, dammit, I might die if you don't!*

She might die if he did. Worse, she might cry and beg him not to leave her, to take her with him, to find a place in his life for her, even if it was only a small place.

But of course he didn't kiss her. He closed the door, leaned down and gave her that familiar crooked grin. And she didn't cry, and she didn't beg and plead. Instead, she got out and stood there, watching him walk around his blasted airplane, undoing the tie-downs, unscrewing the chocks, testing the various whatchamacallits before he finally climbed inside, gave her one last wave and shut the door.

And still she couldn't leave. She stood there beside the gate and waited while he taxied to the far end of the runway. She watched as he came back again, lifted off, circled and headed southwest. She stood there and watched until he was only a faint speck against a cloudless blue sky.

So much for her new philosophy—feet on the floor and cards on the table. So much for reinventing herself. She might as well go ahead and indulge in a messy midlife crisis.

Rafe checked the gauges. He adjusted the trim and thought about the workload waiting for him, the decisions waiting to be made, decisions he had put off for too long. His particular stretch of Pelican's Cove was exposed to serious erosion. Was it wise to invest more there than he already had?

He could love a woman like Molly. The thought broke through his concentration, and he tried to refocus on the derelict hotel he'd recently bought, that he was going to have to either bulldoze or rebuild.

Correction, man. There aren't any other women like Molly.

For the first time he allowed himself to wonder what would happen if he followed his instincts where a woman was concerned. When it came to business, his instincts were superb. When it came to women…

What if he already loved her? How would he know? Could he trust himself to love any woman, especially a woman like Molly, who'd been badly hurt before?

Rafe knew his strengths and weaknesses. When it came to permanent relationships, he dropped off the bottom of the scale. Hell, even his own mother hadn't sent him a birthday card in three years.

On the other hand, he hadn't done a bad job on Stu. The kid still counted on him to come through in a pinch.

Oh, everybody always counts on Molly whenever they need help. Molly's always there. She always knows what to do and how to do it. She's never let anyone down.

How many people had let Molly down besides that jerk she'd married, who still counted on her to pull his chestnuts out of the fire?

"No way, not if I can help it," he muttered.

With no conscious decision, Rafe banked and came about on a heading that took him over the stubby white lighthouse and back to the landing strip. Not that he expected her to be there. She'd be long gone by now, and without another set of wheels, he was going to feel like a damn fool taxiing up Highway 12, trying to overtake her car before she reached the ferry.

By some miracle, she was still at the airport. After making his worst landing in years, he leapt out while the prop was still turning. "Molly! Wait a minute! Wait right there!" She was getting into her car. Rafe jogged across the tarmac and caught her before she could get away.

"Did you forget something? I was going to leave, but—" She broke off when his arms closed around her, smothering her against the hard warmth of his chest.

"Me, too. I would have followed you."

"What made you—?"

He answered without words. A pickup truck pulled into the airport parking area and they moved aside without breaking contact. The kiss said it all. When eventually they came up for breath, Rafe said, "Listen, this sounds crazy, but I've got to make you understand. The kid you must have been? I love her. And the girl you were when you took over the care of your sisters? Her, too. And the woman you are now, and the old woman you'll be someday, clucking over every stray chick and—"

There was such a rightness about it that Molly didn't even bother to argue. Secure in his arms, she said, "Who was it who promised to come back for a couple of puppies?"

"Who was it who paid top dollar for fresh tuna for a good-for-nothing tomcat?"

"Who told you that? It was only a teeny piece."

"I have my sources," Rafe said with a grin that refused to be suppressed. "Ah, Molly, can it possibly work for us?"

"We'll make it work. You know my motto—feet on the ground, head in the clouds."

He still couldn't quite say those three vital words. It wasn't the lack of practice, although he'd never spoken them before. It was just that his heart was still too full. Once he started, he might not be able to stop, and this was no place for a bent-knee declaration. They were already drawing a few leering grins.

But he would spend the rest of his life, he vowed silently, loving this woman. Loving Molly.

*   *   *   *   *

Historical fans, be sure to look for

LONGSHADOW'S WOMAN

*by Bronwyn Williams,
the pseudonym of Dixie Browning
and Mary Williams, on sale
March 2001 from
Harlequin Historicals.*

SILHOUETTE®
MAKES YOU
A STAR!

Feel like a star with Silhouette.

We will fly you and a guest to New York City for an
exciting weekend stay at a glamorous 5-star hotel.
Experience a refreshing day at one of New York's
trendiest spas and have your photo taken by a
professional. Plus, receive $1,000 U.S. spending money!

**Flowers...long walks...dinner for two...
how does Silhouette Books
make romance come alive for you?**

Send us a script, with 500 words or less, along with visuals (only drawings,
magazine cutouts or photographs or combination thereof). Show us how
Silhouette Makes Your Love Come Alive. Be creative and have fun. No
purchase necessary. All entries must be clearly marked with your name,
address and telephone number. All entries will become property of
Silhouette and are not returnable. **Contest closes September 28, 2001.**

Please send your entry to: **Silhouette Makes You a Star!**

In U.S.A.
P.O. Box 9069
Buffalo, NY, 14269-9069

In Canada
P.O. Box 637
Fort Erie, ON, L2A 5X3

Look for contest details on the next page, by visiting www.eHarlequin.com or
request a copy by sending a self-addressed envelope to the applicable address
above. Contest open to Canadian and U.S. residents who are 18 or over.
Void where prohibited.

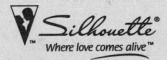

Silhouette®
™ Where love comes alive™

Our lucky winner's photo will appear in a Silhouette ad. Join the fun!

SRMYAS1

HARLEQUIN "SILHOUETTE MAKES YOU A STAR!" CONTEST 1308
OFFICIAL RULES
NO PURCHASE NECESSARY TO ENTER

1. To enter, follow directions published in the offer to which you are responding. Contest begins June 1, 2001, and ends on September 28, 2001. Entries must be postmarked by September 28, 2001, and received by October 5, 2001. Enter by hand-printing (or typing) on an 8 ½" x 11" piece of paper your name, address (including zip code), contest number/name and attaching a script containing <u>500 words</u> or less, <u>along with drawings, photographs or magazine cutouts, or combinations thereof</u> (i.e., collage <u>on no larger than 9" x 12"</u> piece of paper, describing how the <u>Silhouette books make romance come alive for you.</u> Mail via first-class mail to: Harlequin "Silhouette Makes You a Star!" Contest 1308, (in the U.S.) P.O. Box 9069, Buffalo, NY 14269-9069, (in Canada) P.O. Box 637, Fort Erie, Ontario, Canada L2A 5X3. Limit one entry per person, household or organization.

2. Contests will be judged by a panel of members of the Harlequin editorial, marketing and public relations staff. Fifty percent of criteria will be judged against script and fifty percent will be judged against drawing, photographs and/or magazine cutouts. Judging criteria will be based on the following:

    * Sincerity—25%
    * Originality and Creativity—50%
    * Emotionally Compelling—25%

    In the event of a tie, duplicate prizes will be awarded. Decisions of the judges are final.

3. All entries become the property of Torstar Corp. and may be used for future promotional purposes. Entries will not be returned. No responsibility is assumed for lost, late, illegible, incomplete, inaccurate, nondelivered or misdirected mail.

4. Contest open only to residents of the U.S. <u>(except Puerto Rico)</u> and Canada who are 18 years of age or older, and is void wherever prohibited by law; all applicable laws and regulations apply. Any litigation within the Province of Quebec respecting the conduct or organization of a publicity contest may be submitted to the Régie des alcools, des courses et des jeux for a ruling. Any litigation respecting the awarding of a prize may be submitted to the Régie des alcools, des courses et des jeux only for the purpose of helping the parties reach a settlement. Employees and immediate family members of Torstar Corp. and D. L. Blair, Inc., their affiliates, subsidiaries and all other agencies, entities and persons connected with the use, marketing or conduct of this contest are not eligible to enter. Taxes on prizes are the sole responsibility of the winner. Acceptance of any prize offered constitutes permission to use winner's name, photograph or other likeness for the purposes of advertising, trade and promotion on behalf of Torstar Corp., its affiliates and subsidiaries without further compensation to the winner, unless prohibited by law.

5. Winner will be determined no later than November 30, 2001, and will be notified by mail. Winner will be required to sign and return an Affidavit of Eligibility/Release of Liability/Publicity Release form within 15 days after winner notification. Noncompliance within that time period may result in disqualification and an alternative winner may be selected. All travelers must execute a Release of Liability prior to ticketing and must possess required travel documents (e.g., passport, photo ID) where applicable. Trip must be booked by December 31, 2001, and completed within one year of notification. No substitution of prize permitted by winner. Torstar Corp. and D. L. Blair, Inc., their parents, affiliates and subsidiaries are not responsible for errors in printing of contest, entries and/or game pieces. In the event of printing or other errors that may result in unintended prize values or duplication of prizes, all affected game pieces or entries shall be null and void. **Purchase or acceptance of a product offer does not improve your chances of winning.**

6. Prizes: (1) Grand Prize—A 2-night/3-day trip for two (2) to New York City, including round-trip coach air transportation nearest winner's home and hotel accommodations (double occupancy) at The Plaza Hotel, a glamorous afternoon makeover at <u>a trendy New York spa</u>, $1,000 in U.S. spending money and an opportunity to <u>have a professional photo taken and appear in a Silhouette advertisement</u> (approximate retail value: $7,000). (10) Ten Runner-Up Prizes of gift packages (retail value $50 ea.). Prizes consist of only those items listed as part of the prize. Limit one prize per person. Prize is valued in U.S. currency.

7. For the name of the winner (available after December 31, 2001) send a self-addressed, stamped envelope to: Harlequin "Silhouette Makes You a Star!" Contest 1197 Winners, P.O. Box 4200 Blair, NE 68009-4200 or you may access the www.eHarlequin.com Web site through February 28, 2002.

Contest sponsored by Torstar Corp., P.O Box 9042, Buffalo, NY 14269-9042.

SRMYAS2

Desire

July 2001
COWBOY FANTASY
#1375 by Ann Major

August 2001
HARD TO FORGET
#1381 by Annette Broadrick

September 2001
THE MILLIONAIRE COMES HOME
#1387 by Mary Lynn Baxter

October 2001
THE TAMING OF JACKSON CADE
#1393 by BJ James
Men of Belle Terre

November 2001
ROCKY AND THE SENATOR'S
DAUGHTER
#1399 by Dixie Browning

December 2001
A COWBOY'S PROMISE
#1405 by Anne McAllister
Code of the West

MAN OF THE MONTH

For over ten years Silhouette Desire has been
where love comes alive, with our passionate,
provocative and powerful heroes. These ultimately,
sexy irresistible men will tempt you to turn every
page in the upcoming **MAN OF THE MONTH**
love stories, written by your favorite authors.

Available at your favorite retail outlet.

Silhouette®
Where love comes alive™

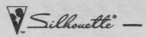